"Close your eyes," Mark said in a husky voice

Judith stiffened, her head automatically lifting in astonishment. "I don't have to close my eyes. I can't see."

His throat tightened as he looked down into eyes as brilliantly blue as his own. "Makes no difference. We can pretend we're dancing in the dark. It's much more romantic that way." He was rewarded as her lips parted slightly in a smile.

"Are you closing yours, too?" she asked impishly.

"Nope. One of us has to steer, darlin'."

She laughed shakily, his sense of humor and his lazy Southern drawl undermining her resistance.

"Now, close those pretty eyes," he urged, catching his breath at the friction created by their bodies.

Then he cupped the back of her head with his hand, and she felt his mouth brush her temple. A maelstrom of emotion swirled within her. What was no doubt only a kiss to him had shed brightness on the darkness of her past....

A new Temptation author, **Binnie Syril** had many articles, reviews and short stories published before setting out to write full-length novels. A voracious reader, Binnie has been creating fantasies since she was eight years old. Speaking as a writer, she says that her characters are very real to her, and that she feels "guilty till I can work out their problems, translating them into romantic conflicts."

The Color of Love, her first book, focuses on "the ability of the human spirit—bolstered by the power of love—to triumph over adversity."

The Color of Love

BINNIE SYRIL

Harlequin Books

TORONTO • NEW YORK • LONDON
AMSTERDAM • PARIS • SYDNEY • HAMBURG
STOCKHOLM • ATHENS • TOKYO • MILAN

With love to my mother,
for all her help and support,
to the "Editorial Bored,"
who have read every draft since word one,
and to Uncle Heshie—he knows why.

FORTY YEARS OF
Romance

Published April 1989

ISBN 0-373-25347-8

Prologue

"YOU'RE LEAVING NOW, Ms Blake?"

Judith Blake smiled at the night security guard, Vince Gilbert, who was standing at the main entrance to the Centre Gallery. "Sure am." She thought about her dinner date with Greg Hollins, her fiancé. "I've got to be somewhere by seven."

"It's just about six now," the guard replied.

"Oh, no." She sighed. "Late again. But at least my paintings are hung right side up, I'm glad to say." Judith laughed to herself, remembering how one of her massive, oversize abstracts had been displayed upside down for nearly a month before a wide-awake curator had realized the painting had been mishung. Hopefully Greg would understand her need to play sidewalk engineer. "I guess I'd better get out of here."

"You drive carefully, now. Have you got good tires? It's pretty messy out there for late March."

Judith flushed guiltily, having no idea what kind of tires her Escort was equipped with. "I promise to drive carefully. You do the same, Vince, when you leave. And meantime, guard my paintings for me."

"Will do, Ms Blake. See you soon."

Judith pushed open the heavy glass door, gritting her teeth at the blast of icy rain and wind that almost pushed her back inside. The guard was right—the temperature had dropped. And thanks to that the cold rain had turned to sleet. Wonderful.

For a moment she thought of going back inside and calling Greg to tell him she'd be late. But that would only earn her a very gentle, well-meant lecture on the importance of being on time, she thought as she slogged to her car, almost slipping twice on the slick sidewalk. And since Greg would have already left the bank where he worked, she might not even be able to track him down and would be even more unforgivably late. Clearly it was a no-win situation, she told herself as she started the car and headed for the suburban Baltimore house where she lived.

It was all she could do to stay on the narrow, winding roads that led to Mount Washington, which was not a mountain at all, but simply a very hilly area of northwest Baltimore. Visibility was poor and getting worse. Beyond the sharp rise just ahead, the road faded into nothingness.

Judith tried to drive as slowly as possible without stopping or braking, but as she crossed the bridge she felt the car veer sharply. Her hands fought for control as the vehicle gained speed on the sharp decline, finally spinning where the road flattened out. Eventually the car ground to a jarring stop against the guardrail and her forehead cracked viciously against the steering wheel.

She shook her head, trying to clear it, trying to stop shaking at the thought of what might have happened—but she couldn't. There was a steep drop just beyond the rail. Her fingers trembling with reaction, she tried to restart the car. . . .

MARK LELAND WATCHED taillights dance wildly on the icy, winding road before him. He focused all his concentration on his driving, tightening his grip on the steering wheel, certain now that he would have been better off sleeping on the couch in his office rather than driving home in this rotten weather. But after coming off a trip to Germany, his first day back in Baltimore had been bracketed with marathon meetings. And now a long-postponed bout of jet lag was starting to kick in. All he wanted to do was get horizontal and sleep for the next day or two, if he could. He had been stubborn, he acknowledged as he rolled his shoulders to ease the growing tightness in his muscles, but all he'd wanted was to get home.

As Mark crossed the bridge on the down side of the hill, the car began to lose traction, then started to skid. He wrenched the steering wheel, feeling a rush of fear when the rear end started to fishtail. He saw nothing ahead—until it was too late.

JUDITH FELT a brief moment of horror at the headlights that were bearing down on her from the top of the hill. "No!" She didn't know if the word was a whisper or a shriek. And then it was too late, and the night was shattered into an infinity of fragments.

SILENCE. That's all there was. No, there was more, Mark realized dimly as he tried to force his mind back on track. There was pain—some bearable, some not so bearable, but all of it was punctuated by the groan of twisted metal. And something else. He struggled for a deep breath, but gave up after feeling sharp pains in his chest. Ribs. Broken, probably.

Think, he ordered himself. Never had his much-vaunted logic been more necessary. Or more lacking. Damn. He swallowed, automatically noting the taste of blood in his mouth. And there was pain in his head—sharp, piercing and insistent. He knew that he needed help. Reaching for the car phone, he punched out 911 and gave the dispatcher the information. That done, he wanted nothing more than to sink back into what was left of his car and wait for help. But something wouldn't let him. Something was knocking at the door of his mind, refusing to let him rest.

The other car. His car had hit another one. He turned his head, but his vision was blurred by the rain pounding against the cracked windshield. A shiver chased down his spine as he struggled to open the driver's door. When he finally succeeded, he was immediately slammed by the fury of wind and freezing rain. He slipped on the icy roadway but kept on going, ignoring the elements and his own pain as he doggedly worked to reach the other disabled vehicle.

It was jammed against the guardrail, half-crushed by his own larger car. The raw odor of gasoline told him that there was a real danger of fire, despite the icy rain. Fear clawed at his insides as he labored frantically to force open the crumpled door. Out. He had to get the driver out of there before the fuel ignited.

Mark fought twisted metal and his own weakness in a painful effort to get to the person. He hurt his hands, but finally managed to get the door open. It was a woman, he saw as he strained to remove her from the potential death trap her car had become. She had blood on her face, and in the dark strands of her hair. "Oh, God!" he groaned. Fighting light-headedness, he pulled her free and forced himself to keep moving until he reached relative safety, away from both cars. He wanted to lift her into the warmth of his own car, but the danger of fire from leaking gas was too great. And he also knew that he didn't have a prayer of getting her to any other kind of shelter; his body would refuse to cooperate. He sank down to the gravel shoulder, panting, extending his arm to draw her close to the shelter of his body.

Cold. He held her closer.

Pain. He staved it off, concentrating on blocking it out.

Bone-deep tiredness. In spite of himself, his eyes began to close, and weariness washed over him in waves. The long hours he had been putting in over the past few weeks combined with the pain and shock of his injuries were all taking their toll. He fought to stay awake, but simply faded in and out.

A moan pierced the fog that threatened to descend. She needed his help, but he had no idea what to do for her...or for himself. He tried to see how badly she was hurt, but stopped when she moaned again. "You'll be all right, I promise," he whispered.

"It's dark," he heard her say in a voice that trembled from pain and fear. It was dark, but not so dark that the blackness was complete. Both sets of headlights were still on, as were the interior lights that shone through the open door of his car. She was in shock, he realized, and being outside in the rain wasn't doing her any good. He looked longingly at the interior of his car, then suddenly damned himself for his own stupidity. Help, though marginal at best, was right at hand. Ignoring the pain the movement cost him, he levered himself away from the woman.

"Don't go," she begged the man who had held her so briefly. She had felt safe in his arms.

"It's all right. I'm just going to take off my coat."

"Why?" she asked, wondering why his voice seemed to be coming from a great distance. "It's . . . cold." He must have been hurt, too; perhaps he was disoriented. Why else would he take off his coat in the midst of all this icy wetness?

"I'm going to put it around you. It'll keep you warm," he said. He draped his camel overcoat around her, then pulled her back against him, resting her head on his chest. "You'll be all right, I promise."

"It hurts," she said, her voice muffled.

"Help will come soon."

"I can't see. *Anything*."

"You'll be all right, I promise." Dear God, don't let me be lying.

How could he be so positive that everything would be all right? she asked herself. He couldn't see inside the darkness. She shook her head from side to side. The darkness hurt, pain lanced through her. "Colors. I can't see them. Oh, my God!"

She couldn't see colors. He, however, saw too much color: the red of blood on her paper-white face, on the dark, wet strands of her hair. If he lived to be a hundred, he would never forget the horrifying vision.

He saw her fingers move toward her face. He grasped her hands gently. "You'll hurt yourself."

"I can't be hurt any more!" she cried.

Smothering a groan of pain from his aching ribs, he gathered her once more into his arms. "You'll be all right, darlin'," he crooned, not noticing the presence of the slight Southern drawl that always seemed to appear in his speech when he was under stress. The words had become a talisman, a litany. If he said them enough times, maybe they would even be true. In the distance, he could hear the wailing of sirens. He hoped the emergency vehicles didn't hurtle into both their cars.

He tightened his hold on the woman in his arms, not wanting to let go even when he felt the helping hands of the paramedics.

The last thing he heard before the darkness descended was her voice trailing off into a desolate whisper. "There aren't . . . any . . . more . . . colors . . ."

1

JUDITH BLAKE HADN'T wanted to go to the Centre Gallery benefit dance. She'd learned to cope with dining out and entertaining at home, shopping expeditions and, of course, her job at Personal Touch answering services. But the thought of walking into a ballroom filled with strangers struck terror into her heart. It should have been the easiest thing in the world to decline the invitation. It wasn't—not when it came from her cousin, Leo Sullivan, and his wife, Maggie, who were Judith's best friends.

"You know I don't like crowds," she'd protested when Maggie had first invited her.

"I know you don't, love, but you won't be with a crowd. You'll be with Leo and me. Everyone else will be irrelevant, except for the orchestra."

A group of *three*. "Oh, Maggie, *please*." Since Greg . . . She gritted her teeth, forcing her mind away from that time in her life following the accident more than a year before. By her own choice, her dates had been few and far between. And more often than not they strained her nerves to the breaking point. "I don't want to be a third wheel," Judith had said finally. At that point she'd been treated to Leo at his most persuasive.

"You're not a third wheel," he had growled via the extension phone. "You're part of the family."

Family. How could she say no to the people who had done so much for her, demonstrating their love and care in so many ways? And maybe the dance would be a way of severing links with the dark year just past, with her broken engagement to Greg, and more than that, with vague remembrances of that awful night that came back to haunt her in fragmentary snatches.

Sometimes she would hear a voice, and think it sounded familiar. Other times it would be a smell, or even the touch of icy cold. She'd never shared these flashbacks with anyone, not even with Leo and Maggie, not wanting to worry them with what she was certain was an overactive imagination. But in the corridors of endless night, it all seemed much too real. If she could only forget all of that, forget about the impossibility of trying to turn back the clock, forget the name of the man whose driving had sent her into darkness, perhaps she would be more ready to face the future....

In the end, she had agreed to go to the dance, which still didn't make her any less apprehensive. Even now her hands shook as she slipped on the Prussian-blue silk gown she'd selected. It was deceptively demure, with long, tapering sleeves and an almost Victorian neckline. The rich jacquard fabric was draped in front to outline the proud thrust of her full breasts, as contrasted with the slenderness of her waist. Yet the back was cut to reveal a glimpse of the elegant line of her spine.

Once she had managed the seemingly endless hooks, she'd seated herself at the vanity in her bedroom. Thankfully her makeup was completed. All she had to do was fasten the long, filigree earrings that had been her mother's. After she'd finished, she reached across the cool surface of the mirrored gallery tray until her fingers located the familiar square bottle of Chanel. The perfume was applied to pulse points at her neck and wrists.

"Done," she said with a sigh as she picked up the beaded crystal evening bag and the exquisitely embroidered black velvet stole that would finish her outfit. Then, pulling a smile out of storage, she went to answer the door.

"You look wonderful," Maggie said by way of greeting. "The dress is gorgeous on you. I knew it would be. Why don't I look like I've just been dressed by Louis Féraud and had my makeup and hair done at Elizabeth Arden?" She sighed.

"I've had lots of practice." If she tried to dress or do her makeup at any speed other than slow, the results were usually disastrous. Judith had learned those lessons the hard way. "You, on the other hand, have to cope with Leo, and Robbie, the seven-year-old whirlwind."

"Ladies, you both look fantastic. You'll be the belles of the ball, and I'll be the envy of every man at the dance tonight, but only if we get a move on," Leo grumbled good-naturedly.

"Yes, dear," Maggie replied in a mock-obedient voice.

Judith chuckled as she draped the stole around her slender shoulders, then tensed as Leo took her ice-cold hand in his and asked her if she was ready.

She took a deep, shaking breath. "I guess so."

"Would you feel more secure if you had your cane?"

The white cane, which was made to collapse into twelve-inch sections, was Judith's trailblazer, helping her get around. But it was also the badge of her disability, even more so than blue eyes that could no longer see. "I don't think it'll fit into my evening bag," she said with a lightness that sounded forced to her own ears. She was rewarded by the brief pressure of Leo's fingers over her own as the three of them left the house and ventured out into the warm May night.

THE MAN STOOD just to the right of the picture window in what had once been the front parlor of the venerable old mansion. From his vantage point he could see north to Cathedral Street and south to the Washington Monument, which was the center of historic Mount Vernon Square. Everyone who walked up the four carpeted steps to the nineteenth-century mansion—now the Engineers Club—passed before him. He felt as if he were behind invisible glass: he could see them—they couldn't see him.

He had no interest in the array of tuxedoed men and beautifully dressed women, until one group of three remarkably disparate-looking people walked through the doorway. The man of the group was big and burly, looking more like a prizefighter than someone who would be attending a charity dance. The lady on his right was slender, her blond, curly head barely reaching his shoulder.

The observer's gaze suddenly narrowed, zeroing in on the second woman. Slightly taller than her female companion, her upswept hair was the color of warm chestnut. He tensed, wishing he dared approach her. He held himself rigidly still, keeping to the promise he'd made. Then he relaxed slightly as the group passed by him. They came through the archway, then into the parlor on the way to the ballroom. She was so near that he could smell her perfume.

If he had any sense he would leave now.

Hands jammed into the pockets of his slacks, he walked through the library, past the wrought-iron staircase and into the ballroom.

"OUR TABLE, ladies," Leo announced as he seated Judith. "I'm going to get us some champagne. Be right back."

"And I'm going to assemble a couple of plates of hors d'oeuvres," Maggie added. "Will you be all right?"

"I'll be fine, Maggs."

"Just so you know where things are, there's a vase with a tea rose in the middle of the table. And at three o'clock to the right of it, there's an ashtray."

"Horrors! Thanks, love." Judith could hear the scraping of chairs and the click of heels as people sat down at other tables, all of which told her that the room was filling up.

"I'm back with an assortment of munchies," Maggie said breathlessly.

"That was quick. What did you bring?"

"Shrimp, raw veggies, toasted Brie." She then told Judith where the plates and cocktail napkins were located.

"Yum. Maggie, you're so nice to share Leo."

"What are husbands for? Speaking of which, here comes our champagne."

Judith heard the brush of fabric as Leo leaned over, setting a glass next to her hand. She wrapped her fingers lightly around the footed stem. "Thank you, Leo."

The orchestra struck up a waltz and Judith found herself humming along to Strauss. "How suitably elegant. When are you going to ask Maggie to dance, Leo?"

He groaned his answer, then rose. "Chivalry is not yet dead. But all I can promise is the box step, I'm afraid."

"I've had my shoes reinforced."

"Go on, you two," Judith heard Maggie sigh.

"You're next, Judith."

"Forewarned is forearmed," she called after them. Suddenly Judith was glad she had come, glad to be out among people. Without knowing why, she felt absurdly light-hearted. Maybe it was because she was dressed to kill for the first time in so long. Perhaps it was the lilting waltz in the background. Or it could have been the champagne that tickled her nose and threatened to make her sneeze. At the moment she didn't know why the feeling was there; she was simply determined to enjoy it for all it was worth.

As she lifted the glass for another sip, she felt the velvet stole slip from her silk-clad shoulders. She hurriedly set down the glass as she reached out to prevent the wrap from sliding any farther. She dreaded the awkward scrabbling around that she would have to do if it actually landed on the floor.

"Allow me," came a deep, masculine voice from somewhere to the left and behind.

She smelled a whiff of expensive cologne as she felt a man's hands put the stole back where it belonged, his fingers brushing lightly across her shoulders as he did so. His touch seemed to linger at the point where the silk fabric of her gown dipped across the sensitive skin of her bare back.

"Thank you," she murmured, working to control a shiver of apprehension as she wondered if he meant to use his good deed as the opening gambit for a conversation. She wasn't much on strangers. But even before her words of thanks had died away, she was alone again, listening to fading footsteps. The man was just a Good Samaritan who was going from point A to point B, and had noticed a slipping stole en route. She had no reason to be concerned or disappointed, Judith assured herself.

More footsteps, and then there was the scrape of a chair next to her own. Two chairs. "Your turn to dance," Judith heard Maggie say.

"Um, no thanks, Maggs. I really don't think—"

"I *do*," Leo cut in deliberately. "Maggie's just gotten me warmed up. You want all this practice to go to waste?"

"Perish the thought." Judith laughed lightly.

And then Leo was behind her chair.

She placed her fingers lightly on his arm. "Nothing fancy, now," Judith warned.

"I'll be good," he promised solemnly. "Besides," he added, "I don't know anything fancy."

"Sure." He was as good as his word, though, holding her close, but not too close, and guiding her carefully and skillfully around the dance floor.

In spite of Leo's bracing words, Judith's heart was hammering as she tried to remember all the intricacies of dancing.

"Relax," he whispered into her ear.

"I'm trying. It's just, well, I haven't done this in a long time, not since . . . since—"

"Since that bastard took a walk."

"Since the accident," she corrected, preferring not to think about Greg.

"The accident," Leo echoed, giving her hand a gentle squeeze. Then he stopped, even though the music continued.

"What's wrong?" Judith asked. "Is my dancing that bad?"

"Someone wants to cut in."

"How do you know?"

"Tap on the shoulder."

"*No*, Leo."

"Judith—"

"I'd very much like to dance with you," she heard a deep baritone voice say. "If the gentleman wouldn't mind."

"I don't want to," she told her cousin. Then, unbelievably, she felt Leo backing away from her. "Where are you going?" she demanded shrilly, a ribbon of panic edging her voice as her fingers clasped his shoulders.

"Only one dance," the intruder said softly.

"Don't worry," Leo said, capturing her hands in his own as he glared meaningfully at the other man. "I know him."

"But I don't!" Her grip tightened. "Leo, don't leave me."

And then it was too late. Judith's icy right hand was captured in a strong masculine grasp. The fingers of her left pushed in vain against the unyielding wall of the man's chest. She was powerless to resist when her hand was shifted to a well-developed, muscular shoulder. The fact that her fingers were biting into that shoulder through the fabric of his jacket seemed to have no effect on him at all.

At first Judith thought she had been passed into the arms of a man who was a stranger to her. All she could tell in that first moment was that he was taller than she, about the same height as Leo, but more compactly built. Only he wasn't exactly a stranger, she realized as she took a soft breath and was struck by the familiarity of his scent. She had smelled the distinctive fragrance only moments before. Her new dancing partner was wearing the same cologne as the man who had picked up her stole. For some reason she couldn't quite fathom, it was a scent that lingered in her memory, holding a hint of spice and mystery.

"Relax," he whispered into her ear as he slipped his right hand behind her waist and swung her gently into the lilting rhythm of the music.

"It's hard for me to relax with someone I don't know."

There was the barest hesitation as he moved her fractionally closer to his body. "I have a cure for that. The name's Mark. Mark—Kendall."

"Mine's Judith Blake," she supplied automatically in response to his easy baritone voice, which had perhaps the faintest trace of the warm South laced through it.

"Judith," he murmured as he held her closely in the security of his embrace.

Almost unconsciously, her death grip on his shoulder loosened.

All the while she and her partner moved in tandem, random splinters of sensation pierced Judith's consciousness. For some reason she couldn't identify, the man tantalized her. There was a kind of ghostly familiarity about the steel-hard muscles that rippled beneath the genteel surface of his evening wear, almost as if something reached far beyond tonight's fleeting act of courtesy, and back into the dark mists of her memory. She had never met him before; surely she would have remembered. "I know you," she murmured, more to herself than to him. To her surprise, she felt him stiffen and nearly miss a step.

How could she? He had carefully stayed away from her. "You do?"

"You picked up my stole," she explained, wondering why he hadn't remembered. How many stoles did he pick up over the course of an evening? He was very chivalrous. Maybe that's why he was dancing with her in the first place. But pity was one thing she didn't need and would not tolerate. It was one of the reasons she was so careful about her dates. But before she could tell him to take her back to the table, he swung her into a turn, then pulled her even closer than before.

"Yes, I did pick up your stole," he murmured, the firm but gentle movement of his hand at the back of her neck effectively preventing her from moving away from him. He felt her flinch, and was himself shaken by her nearness. Her breasts were outlined by the silk fabric of her bodice. He had to resist the urge to draw her even closer to his body. "Now relax and enjoy the music," he urged, his voice a shade lower than usual.

Easier said than done, she told herself as she tried to calm the accelerated beating of her heart. His fingers were slightly callused, but so gentle that she knew instinctively that he wouldn't harm her sensitive skin. She swallowed, shaken by the exquisite sensuality of his touch.

He could feel her tension as his fingers glided across the ivory smoothness of her neck, past silk-covered shoulders, then dipped lower to stroke the satiny smooth skin of her naked back beneath the folds of the stole. "You don't feel any more relaxed," he breathed into her ear, his rapid heartbeat a counterpoint to the ballad being played by the orchestra.

How could she relax when her heart's erratic pounding felt more like a Latin American conga than a slow ballad, she asked herself as she arched forward to escape his marauding hand. She was thwarted in her efforts as silk met silk in a sibilant whisper of fabric, and her taut breasts were sensually crushed against him. "I—I haven't danced in a long time." Her voice was unsteady as she tried to still the quivering tremors that turned her knees to jelly and forced her arm across the back of his shoulder for support.

"Close your eyes."

She stiffened, her head automatically lifting in astonishment, almost as if she could see him as he spoke. Obviously he didn't know that she was blind. And suddenly she was impatient with the pretense. It would be over when the dance ended, anyway. "I don't have to close my eyes. I can't see."

His throat tightened as he looked down into unseeing eyes that were as brilliantly blue as his own. "Makes no difference." The ability to sound matter-of-fact enabled him to continue the dance without missing a step. "We can pretend we're dancing in the dark. It's much more romantic that way." He was rewarded as her lips parted slightly in a smile.

An impish thought occurred to her. "Are you closing yours, too?"

"Nope. One of us has to steer, darlin'."

She laughed shakily, his sense of humor and lazy, Southern drawl undermining her resistance.

"Now, close those pretty eyes," he urged, catching his breath at the friction created between their bodies when she laughed.

She closed her eyes, her mind replaying the warm velvet of his voice in her ear.

"Better?"

"A little," she admitted.

He cupped the back of her head, his large hand gently but firmly pressing her cheek into the hollow of his shoulder.

She gave herself to the sensual enjoyment of music, rhythm and the man in whose strong arms it all came together. It had been such a long time since she'd been held by a man for reasons other than simple comfort or compassion. His touch, as well as the way her body seemed to become almost one with his, made her once more aware of herself as a woman. Newly alive to her own sensuality, she found her hand inching upward from the hardness of his shoulder to the thick, soft hair at the back of his neck.

Her tentative touch sent shivers of awareness racing the length of his spine.

She felt her spirits plummet when the music ended, feeling in advance a keen sense of loss at a lovely interlude being over.

He didn't relinquish his hold on her. "I want one dance all for myself. I don't want to share it."

She wished that the music would never stop as the second dance came to a close. She didn't want to ask for his arm so that she could get back to the table. But when the music did stop, Mark didn't take her back to the table right away. In fact, he held her as if the orchestra hadn't stopped playing at all. And then her heartbeat shifted under a fleeting touch of warmth as his mouth brushed her temple and his cheek rested briefly against her hair.

She caught her breath in wonder at a kiss so light that she might well have imagined it, and yet so achingly sweet that she had to take refuge in his strength to offset the wave of dizziness about to engulf her. A maelstrom of emotions swirled within her as she was torn between wanting the kiss to be repeated—and wishing it had never happened at all. What was no doubt "only a kiss" to him had opened a cavern in the darkness of the past.

Judith knew that the only way she could regain her emotional equilibrium was to make her way back to the real world. And the only way to do that was to relegate Mark Kendall to the realm of fantasy. She braced herself to ask him to help her back to the table. But before she could even get the awkward words past her lips, he said easily, "Would you rather hold my hand, or shall I take yours?"

"I'd like to put my hand on your arm," she responded, extending her right hand slightly.

"It's yours for the duration," he said as he placed her slender hand on the hard muscles of his left forearm.

"I enjoyed the dances," Judith stated with what she hoped was commendable nonchalance as he walked her back to the table. That much was true. The problem was, she didn't want it to end. Now she knew how Cinderella must have felt when the clock had struck midnight and it was pumpkin time. But what difference did that make? She should have been glad that at least part of her ordeal—her venture into the social world—was over.

He winced at the formal politeness he heard in her voice. No doubt that was his cue to end the intrusion into Judith Blake's evening, which he had begun much against his better judgment. But impulse again warred with common sense. And impulse won again. "Would you like to have dinner with me tomorrow night?"

Mark's question was so unexpected that it virtually took her breath away. All she could do was shake her head in the negative.

"Why not?" he asked softly. "You do eat, don't you?"

Judith stood frozen, utterly shocked at his invitation. Why not? *Because I don't want to. Because I'm scared.* Because she simply didn't know him, except as a partner on a dance floor. She deliberately tried to ignore the memory of the fleeting kiss that had so easily wrenched open doors that she had long thought closed forever. Dancing with the man was one thing. It would be quite another to entrust herself to him—to go out on a date with a man that she feared could shake her small, controlled world to its foundations. Before the accident, she'd had her painting—and Greg. Since then... "I just don't go out very often."

"And tonight?" he prompted.

Since the accident, of course, Judith had tended to stick with the familiar, and she was more than a little hesitant to involve herself in new situations—such as dinner with a stranger. With few exceptions, she hadn't really coped with anyone other than Leo and Maggie for a long time. Why had Mark even asked her? she wondered. Was he feeling sorry for her? Greg's defection had left her badly shaken, her self-confidence in tatters. Did this man, Mark Kendall, feel compassion? Did he pity her? And what would they talk about? She didn't even know what he did for a living. What did she have in common with him? And the biggest question of all—why would he be interested in a woman who was blind? Greg hadn't been, she thought dully.

"Tonight was an exception," she finally replied.

"I don't suppose you could make another exception for me?" He saw the tremor in her shoulders and didn't know if it indicated fear, cold or a combination of the two. If the former, he only hoped that it didn't apply to himself. Dammit, he should have known that it would be too soon. He was lucky she had even agreed to dance with him. Logic told him that he was crazy to try to push that luck. The whole thing could blow up in his face.

She hadn't responded to his question. He took her silence for an answer. "Never mind, Judith," he said, his voice quiet as he adjusted the soft velvet wrap around her shoulders. "I'll take you back to your table."

Perversely, she was angry with him for giving up so easily, and angry with herself for wishing she'd had the courage to say yes. "Thank you." Her hand tightened on his arm. Judith said nothing as he led her across the floor and back to the table, her mind occupied in constructing a graceful good-night. However, instead of seating her when he reached the table, he remained standing beside her, his hand on her elbow. "Is something wrong?" she asked.

"Your friends aren't here."

"They'll be back. You don't have to wait. I don't mind sitting here alone."

Well, that certainly showed him! So much for Judith wanting his company, he derided himself inwardly as he seated her. "Do you mind if I sit with you?"

"N-no." A chair scraped, then she heard the sound of shifting, as if he was settling in.

"Thank you."

When he said nothing more, Judith muffled a sigh, not having any idea what to do next. It had been so easy to be with him on the dance floor, when he had been taking the lead. Now they might as well have been strangers who had never met. Whoever would have believed that I'd be terrific on the dance floor, but couldn't hold my own in a one-on-one conversation, she thought, groaning inwardly.

"How do you come to know Leo?" she asked, glad to eventually come up with a way to break the deadly silence.

Fierce concentration enabled Mark to answer steadily. "Oh, I bought a car from him a while ago." That was only part of the answer, but he couldn't bring himself to tell Judith why he'd needed a new car—or why he'd bought it from Leo, who owned a luxury car dealership.

"What kind of car did you buy, Mark?"

"Jaguar."

"Ah." When he said nothing else, she muffled a sigh and took refuge in her glass of now-flat champagne. She didn't care that the bubbles were gone. At least the glass gave her something to do with her hands.

Holding his breath, he braced for questions he was sure would follow. He didn't know whether to be glad or sorry when she leaned forward in her chair and picked up the glass of champagne that was in front of her and took one sip, then another, seemingly unaware of his presence. She was sitting within touching distance, but looked so remote that she might as well have been a million miles away.

Mark racked his brain for something—anything—that would break the awkward silence that grew to ever larger proportions as the seconds ticked by. He didn't care what subject it was, as long as it kept her attention from the subject of her cousin. And cars. "Have you ever been to the Engineers Club before?" he asked, desperately sending up a trial balloon.

"No," she said, sighing. She turned toward the sound of his voice. She assumed that the awful silence would resume.

Instead, Mark began to tell her about the Victorian mansion that was the Engineers Club, of which he was a member. His description included everything from the parquet floors to the intricately carved woodwork to the Stanford White spiral staircase that spanned the house from top to bottom.

"It all sounds beautiful," she said, unable to keep a touch of wistfulness from her voice. "Especially the staircase."

"If there weren't such a crowd, and if you weren't wearing a long dress, I'd take you up that staircase."

He sounded as if he really meant that, she thought wonderingly. "Are you an engineer yourself?"

"Yes, but you don't have to be one to be a member. I've taken the grand tour of this place more than once. I'd love to give one to you. Someday."

Unlikely. Improbable. Scary. She traced the rim of the champagne glass with her index finger. "Maybe."

Encouraged, he said softly, "I don't suppose you'd care to change your mind about dinner tomorrow night?"

Later she would tell herself that it was a combination of too much champagne and the heady excitement of the evening. But for the first time in many months she felt as if she were her own person, more so than she had been since before the accident. Leo was wonderful, but sometimes he behaved more like a Victorian father than a cousin. And her dependence on him and Maggie since the accident had only made it worse. But even more than that, Mark's attention and gentle warmth combined with what she sensed was his very potent masculine virility, making her more aware of herself as a woman than she had ever been in her life. Ever.

When she said nothing, he took her continued silence to mean no. "Thank you for my two dances," he said, his voice tinged with regret as he captured her hand very gently in his own.

Suddenly it seemed imperative that she respond immediately before her cousin and his wife returned. For a moment longer she hugged the decision to herself. Then she threw caution to the winds, giving him the unexpected reply. "Yes."

He raised his head at the volatile word. "What do you mean?"

"I'd like very much to go out to dinner with you tomorrow night."

He barely restrained a sigh of relief. "Thank you."

"You're welcome," she whispered, her breath becoming shallow as she felt the touch of warm, firm lips on the back of her hand, then on the sensitive heart of her palm. They agreed he would pick her up at six, and that they'd have dinner at The Prime Rib. She'd barely had time to tell him where she lived when she heard him mutter, "Damn." She hid her amusement at the obvious disappointment in his voice when he told her that Leo and Maggie were on their way back to the table. She didn't bother to ask why he was leaving just as her friends were on their way back. She was too bemused with thoughts of their date the following evening.

"I'll see you tomorrow at six," he reminded, giving her hand a final squeeze as he rose to his feet. And the fragile bubble of intimacy was shattered. Silence reigned until Leo and Maggie came back.

"Sorry we deserted you," Leo said somewhat breathlessly. "We were on our way back when we got buttonholed into a political discussion."

"My sympathies," Judith said, chuckling, knowing how little patience Leo had for such things.

"How was your dance?" Maggie asked.

"Dances," Judith corrected. "I danced with Mark twice. I enjoyed it."

"You didn't mind that I let him cut in?" Leo prodded, exchanging glances with Maggie.

"I survived," Judith said with a light laugh, her mind still half on their upcoming date. "And before you ask—no, I do not want to make it three. I'm all danced out."

Judith let Leo assume she was too tired to dance any more that evening. In reality, she was loath to obliterate the warmth she'd felt in Mark's arms. She sipped at the last of her champagne and half listened to the conversation around her, presenting no argument when, an hour or so later, Maggie suggested that they leave.

For the first time in ages, she went to sleep anticipating instead of fearing her dreams.

2

YES.

Even now, almost a day later, she couldn't believe she'd said the word. For more than a year she'd led a careful, controlled existence. Last night, thanks to champagne and soft music and the presence of a man she barely knew, she had broken out of her straitjacket with a vengeance.

On the way home in the car last night, Maggie, in a strangely diffident voice, had asked if Judith was glad or sorry that she'd been bullied into coming to the dance. Judith remembered wondering at the time if Maggie was suffering latent guilt feelings because of the "friendly persuasion" that had been used. "Glad," Judith had answered without hesitation in an effort to reassure her friend.

But now the effervescence of champagne was a memory, the strains of music long silent, and she had no clear image of the man in her mind. Judith didn't even know what Mark really looked like. She could have asked Maggie, but then the other woman would have wondered why Judith was so curious. So the question had gone unasked, and all Judith knew about Mark Kendall's appearance was what she had learned when he had held her in his arms on the dance floor. He was tall—perhaps a shade over six feet—and well-built, if her feel for anatomy was standing her in good stead. And he was one very virile man.

Face it, Judith, she thought, laughing to herself bitterly. *Before you walked into that dance last night, you wouldn't*

*have known an impulse if it had bitten you on the nose.
And now look at you.*

She didn't have to be able to see to know that her hands
were shaking as she struggled with her newly washed and
dried hair. To her disgust, it absolutely refused to be fash-
ioned into the smooth, elegant knot she had created with
relative ease the night before. This time she was all
thumbs. Finally she gave up, allowing it to fall over her
shoulders, only managing to tame it into a semblance of
order by using jeweled combs at either side of her head.

She put down the hairbrush, flipping up the crystal on
her braille watch. Five-forty, her anxious fingers told her.
Taking even more care than usual, Judith put the finishing touches on her makeup. Mark was due to arrive at six.

Maybe he would call to say he'd be late, or worse, to
cancel. In spite of the fact that she was drawn to this man
and intrigued by him, maybe that wouldn't be such a bad
idea. The thought had been running through her mind all
day, she acknowledged bleakly. Consumed by self-doubt,
she was more than half convinced that she shouldn't have
changed her no to yes the night before.

At one point she had wished for the courage to call information and ask for his phone number, so that she could
cancel. But he was probably at work, she'd reasoned, and
she didn't know the name of his company. Of course, she
could have called and asked Leo, who didn't know about
the date in the first place. Her nerves twanging, Judith had
rejected all thoughts of outside aid and decided to tough
it out on her own. Which didn't make her feel any less like
a frightened rabbit, she admitted to herself as she went resignedly to her closet.

After the accident, Maggie had helped Judith catego-
rize her existent wardrobe by color, as well as select new
clothes. With Maggie's help, each hanger, shelf, drawer

section and clothing bag was color-coded in braille. But now that she couldn't see, the touch and feel of clothes were even more important to her than their color. So it was with great enjoyment that she put on the lace-trimmed bra and slip, and textured stockings, then buttoned the diagonally draped blouse of bronze silk charmeuse, which she wore with her chocolate velvet suit.

A topaz pin at her throat and matching drop earrings completed the ensemble. She was struggling with the earrings when the doorbell rang. The jarring sound broke off her thoughts. Succeeding with the earrings at last, she went to the door.

"Good evening, Judith," Mark said in that voice she remembered so well.

He caught his breath at how beautiful she looked, poised as she was on the threshold of her house. "You look lovely." She was wearing a softly draped velvet skirt. The blouse, of some silky material, seemed to outline the fullness of her breasts. Her hair was worn down tonight, held away from her delicately boned face by restraining combs. He wondered what it would be like to pull out the combs and run his fingers through the silky chestnut softness that curtained her shoulders. "Very lovely."

"Thank you." She didn't add that she wished she could say the same. "Would you like a drink first?" She felt a shiver of anticipation as his hand gently stroked her cheek, then came to rest under her chin.

"I'd much rather have this than a cocktail," he murmured as he lowered his head and lightly touched his lips to hers. He started to kiss her again, then backed carefully away.

"Mark?" she queried breathlessly as the world spun gently around her.

He had to clear his throat before he could speak. "I think we'd better have cocktails at the restaurant." *Or else I'll never be able to leave,* he added silently.

She would have been happy to delay cocktails indefinitely. But she couldn't tell him that. Instead she said, somewhat breathlessly, "Fine, I'll get my coat."

He guided her to the car, where she was soon enveloped in the comfort of leather upholstery. She reached up automatically for the seat belt, drawing it across her body. But as she reached down to fumble with the clasp, she felt his hand on hers, taking the buckle gently from her. Judith tensed, then relaxed as Mark explained matter-of-factly that the buckle was a bit tricky the first time around. "Thank you," she said softly, touched by his effort to save her embarrassment.

After the short ride to the restaurant, he opened the door for her, taking her hand in his to assist her out of the car.

"I can get out of a car, you know."

"And I can be chivalrous, you know."

"Thank you."

He lifted her hand automatically onto his arm as they walked down the path and into the restaurant. "You'll like this place, I promise."

She faltered suddenly, caught up in an odd sense of déjà vu.

"Is something wrong?" he asked quickly, steadying her.

"No, nothing," she assured him. "It's probably an attack of the raving hungries."

"A couple of hours in this place should fix that."

The restaurant was quiet. She could hear a counterpoint of sounds in the background—the chink of silver on china, the fall of ice from water pitcher into glass, the muted, whispering strains of a harpist playing a lilting classical melody. Their journey ended when she was seated across from Mark on a velvet-covered armchair. Before settling back in the chair, she unobtrusively began "brailling" the area of the table immediately before her, ascertaining the position of the china and silverware. But when the food itself came, she would have two choices, she knew and smothered a sigh at the thought: she could scrabble around awkwardly, or ask Mark for help.

Mark said nothing as he watched, fascinated, the light, sometimes hesitating, but always graceful movements of her hands. How would she know where things were once they were brought to the table? He was torn between wanting to meet her needs and not wanting to make an unspeakable gaffe. The last thing he wanted to do was embarrass her. "Uh, Judith, do you need some help? I mean, should I tell you where things are, move them closer, hand them to you? Oh, hell," he muttered, his voice edged with disgust. "I'm certainly making a hash of everything."

She was touched by the rough hesitancy in his voice and his well-meaning efforts to spare her feelings. "Well, the positions of things on the table are described according to the positions on the face of the clock."

"Oh, you mean caviar at two, and osso buco at four?"

"Whatever turns you on," she said without thinking, then felt the heat of a blush warming her cheeks, wondering if the light in the restaurant allowed him to see it.

"I'm wondering if I dare touch that line with a ten foot pole," he said, humor clearly evident in his voice.

"Not on my account," she parried.

She heard a movement near the table. It turned out to be the waiter, who wanted to know if the couple would order drinks.

"What would you like, Judith?"

"Cream sherry, with a twist of lemon."

For himself, he ordered scotch on the rocks.

And then the waiter brought the menus. To her surprise, she was handed one as well. Her hands shook lightly on the heavy leather volume as she placed it, closed, on the table, remembering the awkwardness she'd experienced with other dates. "I don't need a menu," she told the waiter. "My date will order for me."

"I thought you might like to get the flavor of the selections yourself," Mark said softly. "I called ahead of time and asked if we could have one menu in braille."

She was enchanted by his thoughtfulness. "Thank you," she said, picking up the menu and opening it for the first time. "But even though I can read it, it's going to take me a while to get through it all. It must go on for five or six pages!"

"Seven, but who's counting? Take your time."

She didn't eat out very often, except for occasional dinners with Leo and Maggie. "This is wonderful." She sighed contentedly, her mouth watering as tempting descriptions of chateaubriand, chicken Kiev and rack of lamb flowed under her fingertips. "Help! There's too much on the menu. You may starve if you have to wait for me to choose."

"How about chateaubriand for two, then?" Mark suggested.

At that point Judith heard someone approach their table. "Your drink, madam," she heard the waiter say. He had also brought rolls or breads, she discovered, sniffing appreciatively at the aroma.

"The drinks are here, Judith. Your sherry's at two o'clock. There's fresh sourdough bread in a basket at twelve o'clock, and the butter is at ten."

"Thanks, Mark. You're as good at this as Leo and Maggie, and they've had lots of practice."

"You're pretty close to them, aren't you?"

"I guess you could say that," she said as she munched on a piece of still-warm crusty bread. "Leo's my cousin. I came to live with his family when my parents died. They practically raised me. Leo's ten years older than I, and he's always treated me as the little sister he never had."

"He still does."

"What do you mean, Mark?"

"He's kind of protective, wouldn't you say?"

"He's not only my cousin. He and Maggie are my closest friends. They care about me."

"I can see that," he said softly. "And do you and Maggie go back long, too?"

"Back to college. We majored in art and shared an apartment. One Friday night, I invited Leo over for dinner..."

"Ah."

"The rest, as they say, is history," she finished smugly. Maggie was also her agent, but Judith was not about to tell him that. She didn't want to talk about that part of her life at all. It was a closed book. "And their son, Robbie, is my godchild. He's a terrific kid. We eat out, too, Robbie and I, but his taste tends to run more toward McDonald's," Judith said with a grin.

"I take it you like kids."

"Oh, yes, Mark. What about you?"

"I don't know," he admitted with a shrug. "I haven't really been exposed to them very much. I was an only child. And when I was married—"

"You're married?" she squeaked.

"I was. It ended a long time ago."

"Did you have any children?"

"No."

From his voice, and his terse answer, she could tell that he would entertain no questions on the subject.

"Would you like to do this again tomorrow night?" he asked her.

The question both startled and pleased her. "You don't think that we might be rushing things a bit? We haven't even started on tonight's entrée."

"Oh. Sorry."

"Feed me first," she said with a smile. "Maybe I'll be more receptive when I'm not so hungry. By the way, how did you come to attend the dance last night?"

Mark choked on his scotch, wondering what would happen if he told her the truth.

"Are you all right?" she asked anxiously as she heard him sputter and cough.

"Fine," he managed, taking a sip of water. "Why did you ask why I went to the dance?"

"Well, it was a benefit for the gallery."

"Do I seem like a total philistine to you?" he asked tersely.

"No, of course not. I was just curious, that's all."

His hand tightened around the glass he was holding. "My company has a foundation. We were contacted and asked if we would help underwrite last night's benefit for the Centre Gallery. There are other corporate sponsors."

"I'm sure," she murmured, wondering why he sounded so nervous all of a sudden. Maybe the idea of discussing his charitable contributions embarrassed him. "You're interested in art?"

"And artists. I know what I like," he said with a shrug.

"Are you a collector?"

"I've bought a painting or two. I've seen some of your work on display at the gallery."

Judith caught her breath at the pain the words caused her. Ever since she could remember, painting had been the focal point of her existence, the solace she had sought when her parents died, the joy she felt at simply being alive. Not even her relationship with Greg had eclipsed that. "Yes, I was an artist. Emphasis on the word *was*." Her mind seethed with unalterable hatred for the man whose criminal carelessness behind the wheel had robbed her of her ability to paint—and caused her to lose her sight.

"I'm so sorry," he said, his voice rough with emotion.

"Yes, well, that was then, this is now. Now I help run an answering service for clients who hate talking to machines. I have no connection with art." Judith had no desire to talk about herself, her handicap, what she couldn't do, what she used to do. For some reason, the more open and natural Mark was with her, the more she felt the need to shore up the walls around herself. "Do you mind if we change the subject?" she asked as she ruthlessly crumbled a chunk of the excellent bread into minute particles.

"Your wish is my command."

"Fine. Let's talk about you," she stated bluntly, deciding to concentrate all of her energies on finding out about him, to deflect the questions and turn them back on the questioner. "You obviously know what I do. Did," she corrected. "Why don't you tell me something about what it is you do to keep up the payments on that little gem Leo sold you?"

She didn't want to talk about herself; that much was obvious. He felt frustrated, no closer to her than he had been before he had picked up her shawl last night. He had established no foothold, no real contact. He desperately wanted to do that, but was afraid to push the issue. All right. She wanted to know what he did; he'd tell her. "I'm a systems engineer," he replied to her question.

She cocked her head to one side. "Do you want to translate that into English?"

"My company, Engineering Technology Services, studies small businesses, and works with them on how to help them retool, stay competitive, maintain their share in the marketplace, both here and abroad."

"Are you good?"

At that point the waiter arrived.

"Saved by the food," Mark quipped.

After the waiter had served the entrée, Mark automatically began telling Judith the location of the succulent fillet and the array of vegetables that had been set before her.

"Yum." She sliced a piece of the tender meat, popped it into her mouth and chewed it slowly. "Make that heavenly," she said, sighing as she rummaged around the edge of her plate for a piece of broccoli. "And you haven't answered my question yet," she chided, wagging her fork vaguely in his direction. "Are you good?"

"Good enough that I've been in the business for seven years. And I've had to add staff, and do quite a bit of traveling in order to keep up."

"Traveling?"

"I went to Japan recently—to learn, not to teach them anything, I'm afraid. I've been to Europe a few times. And I've crisscrossed the country once or twice."

"It sounds like you keep your nose pretty close to the grindstone."

"I used to. I've put in plenty of eighteen-hour days, and weeks when I'd travel six days out of seven."

"But not anymore?"

"I still travel, but not as much. Nowadays I'm usually at home more than I'm away. I found out some time ago that there's more to life than work." About a year ago, he added silently, on an icy road. "That's why I hire good people," he continued. "We've developed a profit-sharing plan, so everyone's got a stake in making what we do a success."

"How many people work for you?" she asked.

Judith was determined to direct conversation away from herself, Mark realized. Throughout the rest of the dinner, therefore, he offered lightly casual word portraits of his colleagues at Engineering Tech. By the time the chateaubriand was a fondly shared memory, Mark was certain that she knew as much about his staff as he did.

As the table was cleared of the dishes he debated asking her again about going out with him the following night, but decided to wait until they were out of the restaurant. He didn't want her to think that he was pressing her. Above all, he wanted her to enjoy herself. "The waiter's just about to serve us chocolate mousse and espresso," Mark informed Judith. Moments later, he was rewarded by the blissful smile that graced her lips as she tasted her first spoonful of the airy chocolate confection.

"Wonderful." She paused to dip the spoon into the dish again. "Mmm. Correction. *Sumptuous* is a better word."

"I'm glad you like it," he said softly, taking her free hand in his and caressing the palm. Everything around them seemed to fade with the tender contact, almost as if they were alone....

"More coffee, sir?"

"Judith?"

She didn't want the evening to end. Not yet. Yielding to impulse, she said to Mark, "Coffee is one of my strong points. Oh, Lord, I sound like a television commercial for one of those gourmet coffees." She laughed.

No, Judith sounded wonderful, Mark decided. Until that moment, he had never heard her really laugh.

"Well, I can't promise espresso," she was saying, "but I do grind my own coffee beans and brew them through a Chemex. And I have a bottle of brandy..."

"Sounds wonderful," he agreed immediately. He could visualize the two of them on the floor in front of her fireplace, warming brandy snifters between their hands. Warming each other...

"Sir?"

"Just the check, please," he told the waiter, handing the man his charge card.

Moments later the waiter returned with a discreet leather folder on a silver tray. "I hope you and the lady enjoyed your dinner. The charge slip and your credit card are in the folder, Mr. Leland."

Bells went off in her head.

"Judith..."

"*Leland?*" she echoed with deadly softness.

She ignored him as her fingers frantically searched the table for the credit card the waiter had returned. Just as they came in contact with the leather folder, his hand came down on top of hers, firmly grounding it and the leather folder to the linen-covered table.

"I want to see that card."

"Judith, please—"

"After I see the card."

Reluctantly, his fingers loosened and lifted. But she made no move to open the folder, which lay beneath her fingertips as a kind of flat Pandora's box. She was brutally reminded of the Frank Stockton tale of the lady or the tiger. She might open the folder and find that his first name was really something perfectly innocuous, like James or Michael or Peter....

She opened the folder.

Or she could find out that his name was something else. A name she knew as well as her own. A name she would have given anything not to know, and to be able to forget....

Her fingers unerringly located the credit card. She couldn't tell what company it came from. She didn't care. Her sensitive fingers traced the raised lettering; the name of the cardholder was Mark Leland. Bile rose in her throat. "No." The word was a constricted whisper.

She was sitting across from the one man in the world she had never wanted to see again. No, she corrected bleakly, see was definitely the wrong word. She had never seen him at all. Would *never* see him. But the mere mention of his name was enough to conjure up a hellish, dark void.

"Will you let me explain?" His voice was low and rough.

She trembled with rage as she tossed the card at him, then shoved her wrist through the loop of her cane.

"Wait. I'll help you."

"No!" She heard his chair scrape and, thinking that he meant to stop her, twisted away and almost went down in a heap as the cane became entangled with the table leg.

Strong hands gripped her arm, halting her fall. "Are you crazy? You don't know where you're going!"

"I don't care. Let me go!"

He hauled her, struggling, against his chest. "Stop it." The words were ragged with emotion. "If you want to go home, I'll take you."

"I can make it on my own. I don't want your help. I don't need your help."

He shifted so that his arm banded her waist. Then he scrawled his signature on the charge slip. "We'll get your coat and get out of here."

She said nothing, but walked stiffly beside him until he'd retrieved the coat. She allowed him to help her into it. Anything to end the awful evening.

"Stay here while I get the car," he told her when they'd reached the entrance of the restaurant. "It's raining."

Rain and Mark Leland. She shuddered. "I'm not going with you. I'm getting a cab."

"Like hell," he muttered, shouldering open the door.

She felt the cold air on her face, and the urgent need to get away from him defeated her normal caution. Recklessly, she bolted past him.

He whirled her around so fast that she fell against him, dizzy and disoriented. She struggled against the arm that steadied her as a helplessness she hadn't known since the early days of her blindness threatened to overwhelm her. She hated him for it. "Let me go! I hate you! Don't you know what you've done to me?"

"Yes!" He'd thought of nothing else but Judith Blake for a year. A wave of bitter regret washed over him, leaving him physically shaken. He took a deep breath. "It's only a twenty minute ride. You won't have to endure my company for long."

"You really think I'd ride with you?"

"You drove over here with me two hours ago."

"That's before I knew your track record."

"Christ, Judith!" A stab of pain crucified him. She was frightening him. He couldn't risk driving her home himself. In the state she was in, she just might try opening the door while the car was in motion, and hurt herself badly. "I'll get you a cab."

Her hands clenched impotently into small fists, her nails digging into her palms. She wanted only to be home, away from him, as far as possible from this ravager of her future and her past. Instead, he maintained a hold on her that didn't allow her to move. From where she was standing, she could hear the sound of blowing rain, which graphically recalled awful memories that she had tried so hard to suppress. Memories of pain, cold. She tried to block it out of her mind, but the presence of the man beside her forced remembrance of the night she had first "met" him.

They waited in tense silence until the cab finally came. And when it did they walked into a steadily falling rain. Mark put her into the cab, then got in beside her.

"What are you doing?"

"Seeing you home."

The last thing she wanted was to be trapped inside the cab with the man who would be irrevocably associated with the worst day in her life. "Don't," she moaned.

"Like hell I won't!" He was still hoping that by the time the cab ride was over she would be willing to talk to him, let him tell her the things he should have said when he had first taken her into his arms the night before. There were so many things he wanted to say to her, but he knew better than to try to talk, knew from the stiffness of her body, the pallor of her skin, that she wouldn't respond.

She couldn't risk talking to him, or even listening to what he said. Her control over her emotions was too fragile, her nerves rubbed raw from holding back tears that burned to be shed. Her only option was to cut him dead.

"THAT'LL BE five-fifty, folks."

Before Mark could reach for his wallet, she was out of the cab and onto the sidewalk. His heart contracted as he saw the steep incline that led up to the front of the house. "Wait for me," he told the driver, and started after her.

She heard him running up the walk behind her, sensed his presence beside her just as she reached the front door.

She fumbled for her key, turning it in the doorknob. But she was too late. His hand came down over hers.

"Let me come in with you—just to talk," he pleaded.

"I don't talk with liars. You lied to me!"

"I've never lied to you."

"Not even about your name?"

"I never lied to you. Kendall is my middle name."

"And you never offered to tell me your last name."

"If I had, you would never have talked to me at all."

"Right." She laughed bitterly. "I hate the sound of it. To me, Leland means darkness." Then in deadly quiet tones, she said, "Leo engineered this whole thing, didn't he?"

"He knew I planned to be there last night. Don't blame him. It wasn't his fault. I've been trying to see you for a long time. He always said no, that it would upset you."

"That's an understatement," Judith muttered darkly. "So what happened last night?"

"He figured it would be an opportunity for me to see you—from a distance."

"But you decided to take it further, didn't you, Mark?"

"I thought if I could just get you to listen to me—"

"You should have known better, and so should Leo."

"Are you perfect, Judith?" Mark grated, emotionally at the end of his tether.

"You of all people should know that, Mr. Leland. The answer is a resounding no! Now let me by!" Fumbling with her key, she wrenched the door open and stumbled inside.

Mark stood outside, oblivious to the rain that was still falling. It reminded him of that awful night, and of the cold-sweat nightmares that had plagued him since then. He gazed unseeingly at the locked door that shut him out, then turned back down the front walk to the waiting cab. "Goodnight, Judith."

There was no one to hear him.

3

DEAR GOD IN HEAVEN, Judith groaned aloud as the fragile threads of her self-control snapped all at once. The slow, steady trickle of hot tears contrasted with impartial cold glass as she sagged against the coolness of the front door. She barely had the strength to stand up straight. Her keys dropped from nerveless fingers, and she had to rouse herself, scrabbling around in the thickly piled carpet until she found the key ring.

Determined to shake off the effects of the evening, she went upstairs, stripped off her clothes and showered. But even the constant pelting of hot water couldn't overcome the chill that seemed to radiate through her from inside out. She put on a long-sleeved granny gown, along with the quilted robe that Leo and Maggie had given her the previous Christmas. Then she poured herself a glass of the brandy she had intended to drink with Mark, and sat down in front of the unlit fireplace, barely aware of the tears that continued to fall.

She felt betrayed by all of them—Mark, Leo and Maggie. And even by herself, she admitted in ruthless candor. How could she have had any feelings for this man? How did he have the gall to face her, let alone ask her to dance, and to have dinner with her not once, but twice? What had his purpose been? Easing of conscience? Both Leo and Maggie knew how she felt about Mark Leland. How had Leo dared to set it up? And why had Maggie gone along with it?

And worst of all, why was she drawn to Mark Leland like a magnet, her own senses hungering for his touch, while her mind ordered her back to sanity? Why did it have to be *this* man that made her feel like a woman again?

HOW STUPID he had been, Mark told himself as he walked slowly away from Judith's house, and back to the waiting cab. He leaned against the cold vinyl seat, closing his eyes. He should have listened to Leo and Maggie, who had both told him that if he came to the dance and actually met Judith, he should tell her who he was right off the bat. If he had, she wouldn't have felt so betrayed, so lied to. If he had, the argument outside her house would never have occurred. But then, neither would the dances, or the dinner. He would never have held her in his arms again.

Hell, he had never meant to hold her in his arms at all. He'd had the vague idea of seeing—just seeing—the woman who had dominated his thoughts for so long, and haunted his dreams, turning them into nightmares. He'd wanted—no, needed—to see for himself that she was all right. After that, he would just walk away, out of her life. That had been his plan. But life had a way of cruelly twisting reality, of laying waste carefully made plans.

He had stood there in the Engineers Club, seen her walk in, the elegant silk of her long dress streaming around her as she walked by. He hadn't sat down at his own table, but had kept a discreet watch over hers. Just watching. At that point, everything had still been under control. If he'd had any sense, he would have walked away, out of the room, out of the building. But like iron to a magnet, he'd been drawn even closer. Her stole had slipped, and he'd been near enough to pick it up. Near enough to touch her. To smell the subtle perfume that had wafted up from her slender neck. And he had felt the ground slide out from beneath his feet.

He hadn't bothered to ask Leo for permission to cut in. The thought hadn't even occurred until the moment it happened. He had simply done it, just to get close to her. Just once. It was a fait accompli. But then he had held her in his arms and looked deeply into eyes that could not look back at him. It had hurt to see her—more than he would have thought possible.

She was beautiful. The only trace of her injuries—*only*, he groaned inwardly—were the lovely blue eyes that would never again know and express on canvas the spectrum of the world around her. Her hands—delicate, slender—had suffered no injury, but never again would they wield a brush. Damn. Damn. Damn.

Mark had never found himself in such a grip of emotion, had always prided himself on being firmly grounded in cold logic, the quintessential engineer. She hated him. And he didn't blame her.

The cab braked to a stop, tearing Mark away from his thoughts. Once back in the Jaguar, he picked up the car phone, wanting with every breath in his body to call Judith. He called Leo Sullivan. "I had dinner with Judith tonight," Mark told the other man.

"Considering that she used to get hysterical at the mention of your name, I call that pretty remarkable."

"I didn't use my name—at least, not my full name."

"Why did you have to do that, Mark? What right did you have to take advantage of the friendship we've extended to you this past year?" Leo demanded.

"No right. None at all," Mark answered in a low voice.

"You told me that you wanted to see her, just *see* her. I had misgivings, but I set it up. I almost had a heart attack when you cut in on the dance floor. I knew how she'd react if she knew she was dancing with you. I figured you would have the sense to dance one dance and then disappear."

"We danced twice, and neither of you were at the table when we got back there," Mark muttered defensively.

"She would have been better off waiting there alone," Leo retorted.

"I'm beginning to agree with you."

"Why did you let it go further?"

He had followed an impulse. He, who pursued logical rather than emotional directions, had followed the path laid by his deepest emotions. "I wanted a chance to tell her about that night. To explain. I couldn't do it cold, out on the dance floor. She was enjoying herself, dammit. So was I. And then we got back to the table—"

Mark broke off, unable to explain the feelings that had permeated his being during the brief time he had spent in Judith's company. The truth would have brought all that to a catastrophic end. But what had he achieved, he derided, except the postponement of the revelation by one day? "I thought maybe if I could get her more used to me, she might be willing to at least listen. And tonight it all blew up in my face—it was an unmitigated disaster. It was so bad that she tried to leave the restaurant without me." Not sparing any of the details, Mark doggedly continued on, despite Leo's exclamation of shock. "She wouldn't listen to any explanations, wouldn't even let me escort her into her house. She left me standing outside in the rain."

"And you just left her there?" Leo growled.

"Short of forcing myself on her, or breaking down the door, there wasn't a whole lot I could do. I'd already done enough to upset her. Naturally she never wants to see me again. Oh, hell, she *can't* see me," he groaned. "I thought about calling her, but I know she won't talk to me. You can say I told you so, if you want."

"I doubt that it would do any of us any good," Leo replied. "I'll go see her."

"Ask her if she'll let me talk to her," Mark pleaded softly. "I just want to see her—tell her everything. And then I'll leave."

"I'll try, but don't get your hopes up," Leo said.

And the nightmare will never end, Mark told himself bleakly.

JUDITH WOKE from a half stupor, not knowing why she was curled up in the living room armchair rather than lying in her bed. There was a dual pounding, some of it in her head, and some of it at the front door. For a moment she had a wild, irrational thought that Mark had returned. "Who is it?" she called hoarsely.

"Leo."

Did she want to talk to him? No, she wanted to pull into her shell and shut out the world. But could she? Would she? She drifted to the door automatically, as if sleepwalking.

"Are you all right?" he asked her.

"Sure."

She didn't look it. Her face was pale and drawn, and he could see evidence of tear stains. Judith was more fragile than he and Maggie had thought. Maybe the best thing he could do for her was back off, not push a confrontation. Not now, when her emotions were packed into a powder keg.... "I'm not going to force myself on you, Judith. Now that I know you're all right, I'm perfectly willing to leave."

But, perversely, now that he had come she didn't want him to leave. "No, stay. I'll make some of that coffee you like so much." She went into the kitchen, intending to follow her normal routine. It seemed to take ten times longer than usual because she couldn't seem to steady her hands.

She jumped nearly a foot when Leo took the milk jug from her.

"Sit down, Jude," he said, using his childhood name for her. "I'm going to call Maggie to tell her you're okay. Then I'll make the coffee this time."

She sat down at the round table in the breakfast nook and listened to his brief conversation with his wife. "She's fine. We're gonna have a cup of coffee and talk. See you in a while." And then Judith hid a smile as she heard him say resignedly, "Yes, love, I'll drive carefully."

"Worrywart," he grumbled to himself as he hung up the phone.

"She's entitled," Judith said as she heard Leo puttering in her kitchen.

"I guess," he muttered.

When Leo set the mug of coffee in front of her, she placed her hand automatically above it. The steaming liquid was too hot to drink, but the mug was exactly the right temperature for warming her icy hands on its ceramic surface. From the scrape of a chair, she could tell that Leo was sitting across from her at the kitchen table, as he had so many times over the years. But for the first time she was nervous, felt awkward, didn't know what to say to him. That hurt. And scared her. Because he was all the family she had left.

"Jude . . ."

"Yes?"

"I added sugar and cream to your coffee, the way you like it."

"Thank you." Lord, they were as stilted as strangers.

"I'm sorry that Maggie and I hurt you by interfering in your life. We had no right."

"Maggie's tried matchmaking before," she said lightly. "This time she just picked the wrong person."

"Don't kid yourself, love. This exercise in futility wasn't matchmaking."

"What was it, then?" When he didn't answer, she continued, "You and Maggie knew who he was, Leo."

"I've known almost from the beginning," he admitted.

"He won you over by buying a car?"

Leo slammed his cup down and headed for the door.

She banged her hip on the table in her clumsy effort to run after him. When she reached him, he was standing by the front door. She put her hand on his shoulder and found the muscles stiff and unyielding. She had hurt his feelings, as well as his pride. "Leo, I'm so sorry—"

"Good night, Judith. I'm leaving before I say something I'd really regret."

"No, please. Come back and finish your coffee. I didn't mean it." She held her breath, then let out a sigh of relief as his arm slid around her waist.

"Forget the coffee," he said as he led her to the sofa. "You told us you enjoyed yourself at the dance last night."

Honesty forced her to say "I did—until tonight, when I found out who he really was."

"Neither one of us knew that you planned to go out with him. We only knew that you'd danced with him twice."

"I know that. But there wouldn't have been a plan at all if he'd bothered to tell me his full name," she muttered sullenly.

"Yes, that would have saved a lot of trouble all around," he told himself.

"Why did you set me up last night? I'm asking quietly, rationally, not in anger. Why did you do it?" His arm went around her shoulders, and she felt him take a deep breath.

"First of all, we didn't 'set you up.' At least not consciously. Mark had been asking about you for a long time."

Leo paused to clear his throat. "He wanted to see for himself that you were all right."

"Oh, God," she moaned.

"He was supposed to do just that: look. I didn't expect him to cut in. And I didn't know what I could do about it without making a scene and upsetting you, which was what I was trying to avoid. And then, by the time Maggie and I got back to the table, you seemed perfectly fine. We assumed he hadn't told you his name."

"He told me his name was Mark Kendall. He didn't bother to add Leland to it until tonight," she concluded bitterly. "So now you know all about my little adventure. I'm sorry I blamed you, Leo. It wasn't really your fault. Or Maggie's."

Or Mark Leland's, either. But Leo couldn't tell Judith that. He knew she would never believe him. "We may not have set up the confrontation deliberately, Jude, but I don't think either of us are sorry it happened." And, hearing her gasp of shock, he went on quickly to say that he and Maggie had been worrying about her for a long time.

"Medically?" she asked with a tremor of fear.

"No, no," he said quickly, squeezing her shoulder in reassurance. "But inside you're carrying around a lot of excess baggage. I'm talking about hatred." She was so eaten up with hatred for Mark Leland that it had created an emotional blind spot almost as bad as her physical blindness. "It's like a wall you've built around yourself."

"What do you want me to do, Leo? You want me to pretend it never happened? Pretend that he wasn't responsible for the accident that took away my ability to paint and caused the breakup of my engagement? You want me to love the man for that?" The last words caused her intense pain, even as she said them. "I can't. I—just—can't," she whispered brokenly, wiping at a trickle of salty tears with the back of her hand.

"Don't, honey," he murmured, pulling her into his arms. "Please don't. I didn't come here to make you cry or do anything you don't want to do." He waited until her tears lessened, then took out a handkerchief and pressed it into her hand.

She wiped her eyes, swallowing against a fresh onslaught. "What do you want me to do, Leo?" she asked once more.

"Talk with him."

She shivered. "What good will that do?"

"There are things you don't know about that night."

"What night?"

"The night of the accident."

"I don't want to know. I want to forget. I thought I'd succeeded."

"If you had, we wouldn't be having this conversation, would we? He won't hurt you."

"Any more," she added under her breath.

"At all," he replied just as softly. And then he added, "Jude, the man's been going quietly out of his mind with guilt."

She let Leo's words roll past her, refusing to consider Mark Leland's feelings. What was wrong with his feeling guilty? He had caused the accident, after all. "If it's so important for me to know something about . . . that night, why don't you just tell me yourself?"

He'd thought of it. He and Maggie both had. For a moment he was sorely tempted to put Judith out of her misery. But his telling her wouldn't do that. Instinctively he knew it would only make matters worse. "Maggie and I both feel that you've got to go back to the source, Jude."

The source of all her pain and suffering. Leo and Maggie had done so much for her. And now, for some reason, they thought it was important that she confront Mark. So be it. She owed them that much and more that she would never be able to repay. "All right. I'll—I'll call him," she told Leo raggedly.

"Good girl. I've got his business card in my wallet. I'll put his office and home number on one of your brailled message cards. Just tell him you're ready to listen to what he has to say. He'll do the rest."

"Why didn't he tell me last night? Or tonight?"

Leo shook his head, remembering how he had asked Mark the same questions. "I think he was afraid you wouldn't listen. Would you?" When she shook her head, he ruffled her hair affectionately. "Enough of all this. You need to get some rest."

"So do you, cousin. I can hear the lines creaking in your face." She lifted a hand to brush his cheek. "Would I buy a used car from this man?"

"Boy, that was a low blow. By the way, love, are you okay to stay here? You can camp out at our place, y'know."

She gave him a big hug. "I'll be fine. You just drive carefully, and give my love to your lady in waiting." She walked to the door with Leo, where she put her arms around him and pulled his head down so she could kiss him on the cheek. "Thanks for caring, Leo."

"Same here, kid."

THE RINGING of the phone didn't wake Mark. Even though it was one in the morning, he hadn't been to sleep yet. From past experience, he knew that on a night like this sleep was something he was better off avoiding.

Leo's end of the conversation was short and to the point. "Judith's a little shaky, but I think she'll be okay. I told her

I thought she should talk with you, gave her your number, but I wouldn't lay any bets as to when it will happen. She said she'd do it, but honestly, Mark, I don't know if the call will ever come."

Luck hadn't been going his way. "Thanks for trying, Leo. I appreciate it."

NUMB. That's all Judith felt as she slowly swam to consciousness the next morning. Nothing else. For a moment she lay buried under the mound of down comforter and wondered if last night had occurred at all. With a little effort it might be possible to relegate the whole thing—every point of contact with Mark Leland—to the category of "bad dream."

But then she made the mistake of sitting up. And she couldn't help groaning out loud. Abruptly the numbness gave way to pain. Pounding. Her head felt as if Bruce Springsteen's drummer had taken up permanent residence inside. And her body felt bruised, stiff and achy.

The empty day stretched before her. Between a minimal breakfast of toast and coffee and a forgettable lunch, she strove for normalcy. Trying to convince herself that this was a normal day, she went into her study where she'd had a special telecommunication system hooked up. From there she could handle her share of the answering service calls, taking down messages on her braille output computer and tracking down her clients in their various haunts when necessary. But even a heavier workload than usual couldn't keep her mind from veering off to everything that had happened the night before. By the end of the afternoon she was ready to admit defeat; her concentration was shot. She called Hana Walton, her partner in Personal Touch.

"Is there somebody we can use as backup for me for the rest of the day?" Judith asked Hana.

There was a pause, then Hana came back on the line with several possibilities. "Sure, no problem. Hey, are you okay, Judith? You sound like you're coming down with a heavy cold."

Tears. Her voice was clogged with tears. She cringed at the thought of what she must have sounded like to their clients. "I may be coming down with something."

"Well, take care, Jude. And take the day off tomorrow if you're not any better. We can fill in. Just send me the messages you've got in the system."

"Sure thing," she said, her fingers accessing the appropriate files. "And thanks a lot for this. I really appreciate it."

Now that her business responsibilities were temporarily shelved, her mind focused once more on the past. Except for painful flashes of memory, the night of the accident had been deeply buried for a long time. It was as if her mind was full of holes. The thought of having those holes "filled in" had taken center stage in her dreams the night before. Now her heart beat faster just thinking about what Mark would tell her—how he would fill in the gaping blankness of the holes in her memory. The gaps had left her confused and fearful. Why couldn't Leo have told her the whole story? Why did she have to confront Mark once more? Would total recall destroy the fragile peace of mind she'd carved out for herself? Her unanswered questions haunted her.

And she was haunted by the promise she'd made under duress to Leo—her promise to call Mark Leland. More than once she half extended her hand toward the smooth Plexiglas tray that occupied the convenient place to the right of her desk phone. Seemingly of its own accord her hand pulled back from its goal, her nerve failing her every time. She knew what she would find there: the card on which Leo had left Mark's number. What was the point of calling Mark? she wondered. What could he possibly have to tell her that she didn't already know?

Damn him. Damn Mark Leland, anyway. Normally she had no trouble making a decision. Now she couldn't even decide whether or not to pick up a telephone. She could do it tomorrow, she decided finally. "No, do it *now*," she ordered herself sternly. Squaring her shoulders, she extended her hand once more, her fingers shaking slightly as she read what Leo had typed in raised braille dots.

She dropped the card as if it were red-hot, as if even that brief contact with Mark—the pattern of his name against her fingers—would burn her sensitive flesh. She rubbed her hands together, almost expecting to feel blisters. Instead she felt sweat—her palms were damp. She got up, leaving the card and the man whose name it represented. Wiping her hands on the sides of her jeans, she wished that she could as easily wipe out the memory of Mark, and the last two days of her life.

On the one hand, she had no desire to have any further contact with Mark Leland. Ever. But Leo was special to her, and the promise she'd made to him weighed heavily on her soul as an obligation. Maybe she could call Mark today, get the whole thing over with. Once more, her hand reached for the card with Mark's work number. . . .

SARAH CUNNINGHAM picked up the phone on the second ring. "Engineering Technology Services. May I help you?"

"I'd like to speak with Mark—Leland," Judith told the sultry voice on the other end of the line.

"He's in a meeting. May I ask who's calling?"

"Judith Blake." He was busy. She had tried and failed. She smothered what she was certain was a sigh of relief. "Uh—thank you. I'll call back tomorrow."

Sarah had almost dropped the phone. She knew that name too well. "Wait a minute, Ms Blake." The secretary somehow suspected that Mark wouldn't mind being interrupted.

When Sarah entered the conference room, Mark looked up from a marketing strategy session.

"There's a call for you, Mark."

He looked around the table at the group of people who were reviewing the marketing reports, and then back at his secretary. "Can you take a message, Sarah?"

"It's Judith Blake, Mark."

He dropped the report on the table. "I'll take the call in my office." After excusing himself to the four people who were waiting for him to resume the meeting, Mark walked out of the conference room and down the hall. All the while he wondered if the call meant that Judith was finally ready to listen to him. Once inside his office, he closed the door and picked up the phone.

"Hello, Judith."

"Leo wanted me to call you," she said tensely, her slender fingers weaving in and out of the telephone cord.

"Do you always do everything Leo tells you?"

Ignoring his sarcasm, she said, "What did you want to say?"

He didn't know what he was going to say—he hadn't been prepared for her call. But whatever he came up with, he was determined to say it face-to-face, not via some impersonal communication tool. And equally important were the four people waiting for him back in the conference room.

"Not over the telephone, Judith." He wasn't about to tell her that he was in the middle of a meeting. But more than that, he'd had a memorable taste of her volatile temper the night before, and he didn't intend to give her the opportunity to hang up on him if she didn't like what he said. And most of all, it was somehow important that he see her again. "Would it be all right if I come over to visit you this evening, after work? You said you were good at coffee."

Her hand tightened on the telephone as she heard him use the word *visit* as a euphemism for *see.* "Yes, all right." He asked if six was all right; she said yes. At least she would be getting it over with, once and for all.

He had the silent phone receiver in his hand when Sarah came into his office and closed the door behind her.

"Are you okay?" she asked him.

"Why do you ask?"

"Hey, it's me, Mark. Secretary, person of all work—"

"Surrogate mother," he cut in.

"That, too," she admitted.

He liked her concern. "I'm fine, Sarah."

"About as fine as you looked when you came back from the hospital after the accident," she retorted with an unladylike snort. "You look shell-shocked."

Sarah was far too perceptive. "I met Judith Blake two days ago," he explained, "and had dinner with her last night. And I've made a mess of just about everything, by not telling her who I really was right away." He didn't tell Sarah why he'd hidden the truth from Judith at first. He wasn't sure if he knew all the reasons himself.

"But she just called you."

"Because her cousin bludgeoned her into it. I told her I wanted to talk in person. I'm going to see her tonight, and I don't have any idea how I'm going to say what has to be said."

"You'll think of something," Sarah said.

"Supportive to the end," he said admiringly.

"Always," she said as she left the office.

Think of something. The words echoed in his head as he went back to the conference room. He forced himself to concentrate on the reports being made and the discussions that ensued; his staff had worked long and hard on them. But once the meeting was over, he stayed on in the conference room, his attention focused not on the company, but on Judith Blake.

TO JUDITH, it seemed as if she had waited all of her life for six o'clock to arrive. The coffee was ready—as ready as *she* would ever be. Her palms were damp, and she had to keep reminding herself not to wipe them on the tan gabardine slacks she wore with a black cowl-neck sweater.

She'd been waiting for him all day—yet when the doorbell buzzer sounded, she jumped a foot, then forced herself to let him in.

"Thank you for letting me come, Judith."

She nodded her head stiffly. "You're welcome. I—I'll get the coffee."

He smothered a sigh as he watched her leave the room, gracefully skirting an overstuffed armchair and a table of china ornaments as she did so. She was obviously at ease in her home environment. Which was understandable. It was her own turf, after all. He, on the other hand, was nervous as hell.

Mark paced back and forth, waiting for Judith to come back into the living room, all the while furtively trying to rehearse what he was going to say to her. But when he saw her coming into the room, every coherent thought was wiped from the slate of his mind.

"All right," she said, sighing and pouring him a cup of coffee, then sitting down on the edge of the sofa. "You got what you asked for: coffee, and a chance to speak your piece."

He sat down in the armchair, then picked up his own cup. He took a sip, too wrought up to savor the dark brew. He set the cup down. "You're ready to listen?"

"As ready as I'll ever be," she said, her chin lifting as her mouth tightened.

Was she really, he wondered as he sat almost within reach of her, his hands clasped between his knees. It all boiled down to one chance—his last chance. He shook his head, knowing instinctively that his efforts were doomed to failure. All right, he wasn't responsible for the accident—not legally or morally, or even physically. The police reports had said so. But emotionally, that was definitely another story. Maybe if he hadn't been so tired, his reaction time would have been quicker. And if it had been quicker, maybe he could have avoided the whole thing. Dammit. *If* was such an ugly little word.

Judith tensed as she waited for Mark to speak, but heard only the uneven sound of his breathing in what was becoming an uncomfortable silence. "Mark?"

He took a deep breath. "Yeah. I—I thought that once I saw you, once you agreed to listen to what I had to say, it would be easy. Easier. I guess I was wrong. About everything."

"I don't believe I'm hearing this!"

"Judith, I would do anything—*give* anything I could to be able to change the past, to turn back the clock. I wish I could, but I can't."

"Is that what you wanted to tell me?" she asked stonily.

"Not . . . all." He wanted to tell her that he hoped to see her again—to hold her in his arms again. "I'm . . . sorry."

She had been falling for him, had almost thought herself in love with him. And all he felt was pity for her and guilt for himself. A lethal combination. And he had the nerve to want to use her to help him unload that guilt, and make himself feel better. Nothing on earth could make her do that!

"You want me to forgive you? You want me to cleanse your conscience, pat you on the head and send you on your way like a good little boy? Well, I won't do it! And nothing you can say or do will make me change my mind!"

Her cold sarcasm was salt in an open wound. "This is what you call listening?"

"I'll listen. But I know that all you want is for me to forgive and forget. Well, I can't remember the night of the accident, but the rest of it is what I can't forget. Your name, for one. Leo told me you'd driven the other car. I tried to forget that—I can't, no more than I can forget what it feels like for a twenty-six-year-old woman to be afraid of the dark. Or to have a man say he—" Her voice was breaking, but she forced herself to go on. "Or to have a man say that he doesn't w-want you any more, because he doesn't want the mother of his children to be blind. I can't forget. I *can't*!" she cried.

In an instant he was out of the armchair and next to her on the sofa. He grabbed her shoulders, pulling her almost roughly into his arms, so that she was forced to face him. "Neither can I, dammit!"

"All right, all right," she grated, pressing her palms against his chest in an effort to free herself from his unyielding grasp. "You want to hear the words so badly, I'll say them. I forgive you! Now leave me alone!" She wasn't aware of the tears that streamed down her face.

He was. He wanted to gather her close, stroke the softness of her hair, wipe away the tears. He kept his hands where they were, enclosed on her arms. She had said the words. But what did they mean? Is that what he wanted? A clear conscience to close the door on memory? He couldn't do that. God knew, he'd tried.

Again, she pushed against his chest. "I've said what you wanted to hear. Now let—me—go!" she panted.

"When I'm finished," he growled, giving her a little shake. "The accident was awful, the worst thing that ever happened to me."

"To you!" She laughed bitterly.

"Yes! I still have nightmares about it. I had to practically watch what happened to you. I saw your headlights at the bottom of the hill, but my car followed the same path as yours, right down the grooves in the ice. And all the time it was as if I were trapped in some awful horror movie where the action was all in slow motion. No matter what I did, I couldn't stop it. I couldn't do a goddamned thing!

"I talked to the police. Your car had done a 360. There was nothing I—or anyone—could have done to avoid plowing into you. It happened. God, I wish I hadn't been driving that day, or that I hadn't been so tired from jet lag. Maybe it would have made a difference. I don't know. But I do know what it's like for a twenty-six-year-old woman to be afraid of the dark. I was *there*."

For a moment his vision blurred, merging past and present, and trapping him once more in an icy nightmare of pain, anguish and fear. "I shared your fear of the dark that night—and all these nights afterward. I held you in my arms. You clung to me, and I promised you that everything would be all right. Oh, God," he groaned.

She didn't say anything. She couldn't. Mark's voice sounded as if it were coming from a distance. She felt as if everything had turned inward, gone black—even blacker than before. Inside she was shaking.

"Are you all right?" he asked softly.

She was sitting on the sofa, her hands clenched into fists, her mind struggling to accept the enormity of what he had said. "Fine," she answered automatically. "I'm fine."

He knew then that he would never get through to her, that there was no point in trying anymore, no point in even finishing the story he had started. It wouldn't make any difference. He had caused her enough pain already. His efforts at making contact with her had caused more harm than good—to her, and to himself.

"I don't expect you to forget. And the word *forgive* isn't part of my vocabulary any more than it's part of yours. I can't forgive myself. I don't suppose I ever will," he said, bitterness and regret roughening his voice as he turned toward the door. He paused briefly, needing to say one more thing, even though it might make her hate him even more. "As for your—fiancé," he added contemptuously. "Breaking the engagement was his loss, not yours. He wasn't worth one of your tears. Hell, you got off lucky. You might have married the bastard. Goodbye, Judith." At least this time she had heard him say the words, he told himself as he opened the door and walked out. He didn't look back.

His words played and replayed in her head, in ever-tightening concentric circles.

She heard the front door open. "Mark, wait—" She got up to follow him. The words, drawn out of her sandpaper-dry throat, were softer than a whisper. Her feet felt as if they were moving through quicksand.

She reached the front door just as it closed.

She pulled it open, standing in the chill air, calling his name again.

She heard his footsteps pounding down the steep front walk, then heard the sound of his car engine. She closed the door, leaning against it wearily.

Too late, her mind taunted. Too late....

4

"MORNING, MARK."

Mark Leland looked up as the door to his office opened and Sarah Cunningham greeted him with her usual bright smile. He had to exert more than the usual effort to return the greeting. "Morning."

She frowned, noting that Mark's appearance was totally out of kilter. He usually came to work in a suit or, at the very least, well-pressed slacks and a sport jacket. His thick, dark brown hair was always well combed, his face clean-shaven. Today he was wearing slacks and a shirt that looked as if they'd been slept in. His hair looked as if it'd been combed with a rake, and his face could have been used in a Don Johnson look-alike contest. A glance around the room revealed the array of coffee cups, the suit jacket tossed on the chair, the scattering of papers on the low table in front of the sofa. "Have you been here all night? If you needed help, you should have called me."

"I wasn't here all night." Just most of it, he added wryly to himself. "And I always need you, Sarah, but all I was doing was prepping for a trip."

"What trip?" she asked curiously. "The only one on tap is Scott's visit to that plant in Michigan."

"Yeah, well, I told him I'd take Michigan, and he can deputize for me while he waits for the big day."

Scott McNeil's wife was pregnant, true, but the baby wasn't due for two months. And Mark hadn't traveled in quite a while. None of it added up.

Sarah Cunningham had worked for Mark Leland for seven years, ever since he'd gone into business for himself. She knew something was wrong, but she also knew better than to pry. She suspected it had something to do with his visit to Judith Blake the day before, and she had to bite her tongue to keep from asking how it had gone. From the way Mark looked—not at all well. "Should I call the travel agent?"

"No, I called the airline last night and packed before coming to the office. All I have to do is shower and change, and I'm out of here," hoping that the change of scene would get him back on an even keel. In any case, a site visit would be a challenge, he told himself, just the thing he needed to occupy—or divert—his mind.

JUDITH'S SLEEP was plagued by nightmares—not about the accident, but about Mark Leland. His words had filled in the Swiss cheese of her mind, linking together glitches and gaps of memory that had too often flashed unbidden across her unconscious, leaving her confused and fearful. Now her heart beat faster at what else Mark might have said if she hadn't been too near shock to respond to the things he'd told her.

She could remember the sound of his voice, recall the pain laced through it—pain she had caused by her callous refusal to listen to him. She'd never consciously hurt another person before. She didn't know how to handle it. Clearly he'd suffered as much as she in his own way. Who had been there to comfort him after the accident? And who was there to comfort him now?

Questions, she muttered as she dragged herself wearily from the bed. And the only way to get answers would be to go back to the source. Her heartbeat almost suffocated her when she picked up the phone and dialed his home number. A machine answered. Hating the impersonal contraptions as much as her Personal Touch clients did, she hung up without leaving a message. But after forcing down dry toast and gulping down scalding hot coffee, she decided to try again, this time calling his office.

"Mr. Leland isn't in," the voice of Mark's secretary informed Judith.

"In other words, he won't take my call," Judith said, not bothering to mask the sarcasm edging her voice.

Sarah Cunningham stiffened at the undeserved slight to the man she worked for. "He isn't like that. He doesn't duck telephone calls." And then, because she knew who belonged to the voice on the other end of the line, Sarah pursued the issue. "He'll be out of town for a few days. I'll be glad to take your name and number."

"Please ask him to call Judith Blake," she said, then reeled off the number for her private line. And then Judith hung up the phone with a sigh, privately doubting that she would ever hear from Mark again.

SOMEHOW JUDITH MANAGED to get through the days that followed, her heart skidding to a halt every time the number on her private line rang. Her impulse was to hide, retreat, forget. But that was impossible. She couldn't hide from herself. And she had a business to help run and a family that cared about her.

It helped, at least a little, when she tried to lose herself in her work. But her nerves were scraped raw whenever she relived the confrontation with Mark. She couldn't forget what she'd said, how she'd acted. And then she went to Leo and Maggie's house for potluck dinner the following Sunday.

During the meal itself, the conversation was light, ranging from Maggie's newest client to Leo's expansion of his sales force. His newest "salesman" was a woman.

"About time," Judith commented. "And speaking of time, who's on tap for next Friday?"

"Next week?" Maggie queried.

"It's your ninth anniversary, unless my calendar and my memory are lying. Any plans?"

"We were thinking of dinner and dancing in D.C."

"What about me?" Robbie piped up.

"You get to stay here, sport," his father replied.

"Aw, gee."

"With me, Robbie," Judith inserted. "We'll have our own little party, do all kinds of things."

"I think I can feel my hair turning gray," Maggie groaned.

"Too bad, Maggs," Judith replied with a grin. "When the cat's away..."

"I get the message," was Maggie's mock-stern reply.

Later, after Robbie was in bed, Maggie asked if Judith was really sure about the baby-sitting commitment.

"Do you trust me?" Judith asked in a low voice.

"Of course we trust you, idiot!" came Maggie's unhesitating reply. "It's just, well, you've been kind of low."

'And you barely ate enough to keep alive tonight," Leo muttered. "And you look kind of..."

"Gee, thanks, you guys. I guess it's been that kind of week," Judith said, taking a deep breath. "You wanted me to talk to Mark," she began reluctantly. "Well, I dredged up my courage." And then, not sparing herself, she related what had happened the week before, how she'd had a vicious retort for everything he'd said—tried to say. And how she wished with all her heart that she'd listened to him. "And now it's too late," she concluded brokenly.

"Leo, why didn't you tell me what really happened the night of the accident?"

He sighed heavily. "Well, at first I thought it was Mark's fault, just like you did. Hell, I wanted to tear him apart. But then I talked to the police, read the reports."

"Mark said my car did a 360."

"Yeah. Dammit, Jude, they never should have allowed that road to stay open that night. They're lucky there haven't been any fatalities there. A thin coating of ice on that downhill, and you're on a glass mountain. Neither one of you had a chance."

"And Mark was hurt himself," Maggie added.

Judith felt a shiver trail down her spine. "I didn't know." The words came out in a whisper. "Mark didn't tell me. Was he hurt—badly?"

"Bad enough to put him in the hospital and keep him there for a while," Maggie replied. "Besides all kinds of cuts from broken glass, he had broken ribs, a punctured lung and a concussion. But in spite of all that, he managed to get you out of your car. When the paramedics got there, he was holding you in his arms."

"I remember someone holding my hands, talking to me. Everything was confused . . ."

"By the time help came," Leo put in, "you were in shock. He was more than halfway there himself. And the cars were both flaming wrecks."

"My God!" She shuddered as Leo's words sank in.

"You were taken to different hospitals," he continued. "Mark contacted me through the police. He also came to see you in the hospital, but I wouldn't let him. Every time I tried to talk to you about the accident, you became extremely upset."

"That's a nice way to put it," Judith snorted. "I became flat-out hysterical at the mention of his name."

"Yeah, well, that's why we never told you any more about that night," Leo said. "Your doctors and the rehabilitation psychologist advised against pushing it."

"And I wouldn't listen—really listen—to Mark, either," she murmured. "I think he told me what he did—the bare bones, not the heroics—because I made him angry. God, the things I said to him!"

"You were hurting, love. And, well, to be honest, I don't think Mark would've told you about the heroics. He isn't the kind of guy that would blow his own horn. Anyway, he's been keeping in touch with us all this time."

And Mark had been going quietly out of his mind with guilt. That's what Leo had said when he'd come to her house to comfort her, the night she'd found out who Mark really was. "Oh, Leo," she said, sighing, swallowing hard. "I don't know what to do, or even what to feel anymore. I've made such a mess of everything."

"Have you thought about talking to your rehab psychologist?"

Sherry Ellison, Judith thought. "Maybe. She was a tremendous help in getting me back on my feet. I could try to see her this week, if she can fit me in. And in the meantime, thanks for listening, you guys."

"Hey, what's a family for?" Maggie asked, giving Judith a hug.

THE FOLLOWING Monday morning Judith found herself in a corner of Sherry Ellison's plush, comfortably furnished office.

"You wanted to talk about the accident?" Sherry asked.

Judith took a deep breath. "I—I met Mark Leland."

"How was it?"

"Until I found out who he really was, it was pretty wonderful." Then, leaving out the intimate details, Judith told the other woman all that had happened since the night of the dance at the Engineers Club.

"How do you feel about Mark Leland then—and now?" Sherry wanted to know.

Judith leaned back against the sofa where she was sitting, her fingers twisting together as she considered her answer. "I know how I used to feel. I used to think that he was a horrible man who was guilty of a terrible crime. Against me, personally. I blamed him for what happened to me."

"You hated him," the therapist said quietly.

"Yes," Judith whispered. Hatred for Mark-as-villain had been her anchor, her compass, a focal point for her existence. It had given her life direction. Everything had begun and ended with him. And strangely, she admitted to herself dazedly, it still did....

"There's no one to blame any more, is there, Sherry?"

"I think you know the answer to that, don't you?"

"Yes, I guess I do. Only God."

"That's right, Judith. And you're going to have to work on getting in touch with yourself, and with the grieving process, all over again, because now you see it from a different perspective."

"And then what?" Judith asked tiredly, her chin resting on her hand.

"And then you pick up the pieces and start living—really living—again."

"How do I do that without being able to paint?" Judith demanded.

"I don't know," came the reply. "I didn't have an answer for you when you asked me that almost a year ago, and I don't have one now. All I can say is, things change, just like your view of the accident."

"You're saying that my view of art will change, too?"

"I'm saying that you have to look inside yourself to find the answers, Judith. Explore the possibilities that were closed to you because you weren't ready to face them. You know, when trauma occurs we become very self-centered. Trauma such as the accident, and the blindness that followed, upset the natural order of things in your life, threw you off balance."

"The question is, what do I do now?"

"Try to regain that balance. Don't close yourself up into a cocoon. Allow yourself to open up to other people."

"In other words," Judith said, taking a deep breath, "accept the fact that I'm not the only one in the world who has suffered pain, that someone else might be hurting just as badly."

"That sounds like a pretty big breakthrough," Sherry agreed softly.

"And what should I do about Mark?" Judith asked after a long moment of silence.

"What do you think you should do?"

"Apologize."

"Then do it. Confront the guy."

"I tried that. I called him last week. His secretary said that he's out of town. He hasn't called back. I don't think he will."

"You don't know that. Give it some time. And take some time to sort things through. Look inside yourself. You've got a new perspective on what happened to you. Now maybe you can really come to grips with it all. Then when you're ready, see him."

"What if he won't see me? I've hurt him, Sherry. I've treated him as if he didn't have any feelings."

"You have to try. And if it doesn't work—"

"I'll try again," Judith said decisively. After all, he'd tried to get through to her more than once.

IT HAD BEEN a good trip, Mark thought as he walked into his Engineering Tech office on a clear Thursday morning. Thanks to on-site management, employee cooperation and Scott's able preliminary work-up, the small manufacturing firm in upstate Michigan would not go under and seemed to be well on the road to recovery. And just before his return to Baltimore, he'd learned that his own company had just been awarded a major reorganizational contract in northern Virginia.

"Welcome back, Mark," Sarah Cunningham said as she handed her boss a sheaf of messages.

"Thanks, Sarah. Good to be back. Give me a few minutes, and we'll play catch-up on what I've missed," he said absently, intending to sort out those messages marked urgent.

"The one on top is from Judith Blake," his secretary murmured softly before discreetly turning her attention back to her word processor.

He stiffened, then walked slowly into his office, closing the door behind him. Why had she called? he wondered, his mind a complete blank. Then he picked up the phone. There was only one way to find out.

"What can I do for you?" he asked formally when he heard Judith's voice on the line.

Her heart sank as she heard the cold stiffness in his voice—so different from the way she was used to hearing it. She had heard it gentle, teasing, angry, and anguished. But now it was cold. Dead. As if it reflected her own emptiness. "I'd like to talk to you."

"It's all been said."

"No, it hasn't, Mark. You could come to my house. Or I'd meet you anywhere you say."

"I've been away from the office for nearly two weeks. I've got a lot of work to catch up on."

Her heart sank. "In other words, your answer is no."

"I don't really see the point. We've been through it all before."

It was no more than she'd expected, but the reality was hard to take. He was unwilling to listen to her, as she'd refused when he had virtually begged her to hear him out. It was poetic justice, she thought dully. "I'm sorry to have bothered you."

At first he felt guilty for not listening to her, and for lying to her. He flicked a glance at the nearly bare surface of his desk. He had hardly any work to catch up on; almost everything in the company was up-to-date and on an even keel. But he assuaged his guilt, telling himself that Leo or Maggie had probably instigated Judith's call. Mark forced himself to concentrate on the few files that needed his attention, channeling his thoughts in other, less painful directions.

Judith held the silent receiver in her hand long after Mark had hung up. She didn't want it to end there, even if he never wanted to see her again. And why should he, after all she had said and done?

The day stretched before her, her mind focused on how she had found a brief taste of heaven in a stranger's arms, only to find that it led straight to a hell of her own making. Judith's instinct was to seek oblivion in work. But then she remembered her conversation with Sherry Ellison—and the therapist's advice: confront him.

Somehow, that gave her the courage to try to talk to Mark once more, determined not to let her case go unheard. But this time she would do it face-to-face, she decided, so he couldn't hang up on her. Surely he owed her that much; she had allowed him into her house to talk to her, after all.

BY FOUR O'CLOCK Judith was in a cab on the way to his office. Giving the driver the address had been difficult. And physically braving Mark's wrath on his own turf was going to be even worse, Judith knew. But she was determined to try to talk to him once more, no matter what the emotional cost to herself.

The cabdriver kindly guided Judith to the front of Engineering Technology Services. She stood just inside the entrance, uncertain how to proceed. She had no idea how big the place was, or what eyes would be watching her make a fool of herself.

Sarah Cunningham looked up from her word processor as the office door opened. She saw a stunningly dressed woman standing in the doorway. She wore dark glasses and carried a white cane. Sarah had a very good idea who the woman was. "May I help you?"

Judith turned toward the owner of the voice she'd heard on the phone. "I hope so." She took a deep breath. "My name is Judith Blake. I'd like to see Mark Leland."

"Mark is in conference, but he should be free in about half an hour. Can you wait?"

"Yes," Judith replied without hesitation.

"Would you like to sit down, Ms Blake?"

"Love to."

"Shall I take you through our obstacle course?"

The woman was sensitive. "If I could just have the loan of your arm . . ." Judith began.

"My pleasure," Sarah murmured as she showed Judith Blake to a comfortable chair in the reception area. "I'll let you know as soon as Mark is free."

"Thank you," Judith said, her hands automatically folding up the cane. "But could you not tell him that I'm here? I mean, could you just show me into his office when he comes back and let me take it from there?"

It wasn't exactly a usual request, and Sarah's job was to protect her boss's time and interests. But some days she operated on pure instinct; today was one of those days. "I'll be glad to show you into his office later on. In the meantime, can I get you anything? Coffee or tea?"

"No, thank you." Judith doubted whether her icy hands would even be able to hold a cup. And the last thing she needed was to walk into Mark's office with coffee stains all over her.

She sat on the couch, her mind trying to come up with a way to convince Mark to listen to her. Lord, the abuse she had heaped on the man's head. That would certainly not make him overly anxious to listen to her explanation, or her pitifully inadequate attempt at an apology. He hadn't even wanted to talk to her on the phone. Would facing him in person soften his attitude? She took a deep, painful breath and wondered if things could ever be made right again.

She clasped her hands together. Her palms were damp. She wiped them furtively on the sofa cushions, then snapped open the crystal on her watch. Four-thirty. When she read the dial again, eight minutes had passed, then ten. For Judith, time crept by on leaden feet, but for the rest of the world, life went on as usual. The phone rang. The secretary answered it, took messages, routed calls. Before Judith could snap open the crystal again, though, she heard the woman call in that Mark was free.

"Calm down," Judith told herself as she tried to steady her breathing and fight off encroaching tendrils of fear. Now that she'd come this far, she didn't want to lose her nerve. She got up as she heard the secretary walking toward her. Moments later she was being guided out of the reception area, more than glad to have the support of the woman's arm. Her own hand was shaking so hard that she wouldn't have been able to use the cane effectively.

"Mr. Leland, there's someone here to see you."

"I didn't think I had any more appointments..." His voice trailed off as he looked up and saw the woman who was standing next to Sarah. "Judith."

"Mark," she said, nodding in the direction of his voice.

He glared at his secretary, who stood her ground. Obviously Sarah had taken it upon herself to decide that seeing Judith would do him some good. Now he understood something of the frustration Judith must have felt at her friends' machinations. "That will be all, Sarah," he said as he placed Judith's hand on his arm.

As Mark guided her into his office, Judith's senses registered the deeply carpeted floor, the comfort of the armchair in which he seated her, the smooth solidity of the flat, wooden surface she encountered when she extended her hand.

"I've seated you across from my desk," he told her as he watched her acclimatize herself to her surroundings. "Why did you come here?" he asked as she placed the folded cane on the floor beside her chair.

She heard the strain in his voice. "Ever since you left my house that last night, I've been trying to figure out what to say to you and how to say it. Everything I came up with seems pitifully inadequate, even to me. I'm sorry for not listening to you after dinner, and when you came to my house the next night."

He made no response.

The silence that blanketed the office was so heavy that she could hear her heart beating. "Mark?"

"There's no point to this," he said tiredly.

"You're saying you won't listen to me."

His feelings had long since been rubbed raw. "I'm saying I'm human, Judith. I'm not mad at you. I just can't take the histrionics—this emotional merry-go-round—anymore. I'm dizzy from it."

"I—I know I have no right to hope that you'll accept my apology, especially when I threw your words back in your face time and time again. But you were wrong, Mark. The word forgive *is* part of my vocabulary."

"So you're ready to forgive me now?" he asked cynically.

"I'm not talking about forgiving *you*. Now it's myself I can't forgive, because of the things I've said and done."

"Did Leo persuade you to come here?"

"He doesn't even know that I came. No, you're the one that did the persuading, when we talked at my house."

"Is that why you said nothing afterward? Give me a break!" he retorted as he pushed his chair back abruptly. He turned his back on her and strode to the wall of windows behind his desk, his eyes unfocused, his mind floating.

Judith winced at the bitter cynicism she heard in his voice. His mind was closed, made up in advance. She knew she was lost, finished before she'd even started. And she realized that it was no more than she deserved. Her sensitive ears told her that his voice was coming from across the office, to the right. She was tempted to turn and try to find her way to the door and leave. But she couldn't, not until she had given it one last try.

Was this how Mark had felt when he'd tried to talk to her, and she had rebuffed him? Raw, helpless, frustrated? "I'm not leaving until we've talked, Mark. Really talked," she vowed.

"I think we've said all there is to say. I can't see any point in rehashing it anymore. All we'll be doing is inflicting more hurt on each other, and that's what we've been doing right along."

Judith ignored the starkness of his words, concentrating instead on the pain threaded between the lines. She felt his pain—it was linked by an open conduit to her own. Tears fell from her eyes as she got unsteadily to her feet, gathering the tattered shreds of her dignity around her like a cloak. She didn't know if he would listen, but she was determined to try once more.

Not bothering with the cane, she felt her way around the desk, heading in the direction she had last heard his voice. Did he realize that unless he spoke, she had no point of reference, no way of knowing where he was? Did it make a difference to him? she wondered morosely. She concentrated, trying to filter out background traffic sounds so that she could home in on his ragged breathing. If she could just reach him, make him face her, maybe she could get him to listen.

Moving silently, she worked her way toward him, her heart shifting into double time. You can do it, Judith, she told herself. You've faced the unknown before. She stayed close to the massive piece of furniture, feeling as if she were once again a child playing "pin the tail on the donkey." It would be hard, she knew, because Mark didn't want to be found.

Mark turned, appalled to see Judith coming toward him. "Judith, no!"

She heard his words, but was determined to reach him. Instead, she crashed into some low piece of furniture, giving an unwilling cry of pain as she went down in an ignominious heap.

She was sprawled on the carpet, at the base of the table that held his computer. In his frantic effort to reach her he almost tripped over the damned thing himself.

"Are you all right?" he asked, sliding an arm across the small of her back as he helped her into a sitting position.

The initial pain she had felt was more shock than anything else, and was rapidly fading into a combination of embarrassment and humiliation. *Judith Blake—royal klutz.* She was conscious of his supportive arm, and had to fight the desire to let her head fall back into the hollow of his shoulder and simply remain where she was. "I'm fine."

She looked unbelievably fragile, he thought, emotion catching in his throat. "I'm going to pick you up, Judith."

"I can get up by myself."

"I know you can." He slid his arm more firmly across her back, slid the other under her knees. "Put your arms around my neck." When she had done so, he began picking her up.

She gasped, tightening her arms around his neck as he lifted her from the floor.

"Don't worry, I won't drop you," he said as he walked slowly across the room.

"I know." She wasn't worried. She was dizzy, but she didn't know if she was disoriented at being off the ground, or from being held against his chest in the security of his arms.

"Do you want to lie down or sit up?" he asked as he approached the couch. If he were to have his wish, she would want to stay right where she was. Not bloody likely, he realized grimly. Either way, she was more than vulnerable to him.

"Sit, please."

Placing her very gently on the couch, he retrieved a throw pillow and placed it behind her back. "What hurts you?"

Inside or outside? she wanted to ask. "My shins, and my left arm," she told him finally.

He knelt before her, running his hands over the twin depressions of dark redness that scored both of her lower shins. Both places would ripen into nasty, deep bone bruises later.

"Am I black and blue?" she asked, forcing herself not to flinch at the gentle warmth of his touch.

"You will be."

"Blind people are used to bruises." She heard the indrawn hiss of breath to her left, and knew that she'd hurt him again. "Oh, Mark, I'm sorry." She turned, reaching out, one hand finding and grasping his upper arm, the other, palm outward, colliding with his chest. "Just— sorry," she managed brokenly.

There was no sound, just the sensation of her fingers on his flexing biceps, her palm flat against the erratic thudding of his heart.

He looked at her downbent head, swallowing against the erotic sensations unconsciously created by her touch. He could only guess at how difficult it must have been for her to come and face him. And then his reception had not been unwelcome, it had been downright hostile. And still she had tried to reason with him. He had stonewalled her—shut her out—stopped speaking, so that when she had tried to find him, she'd been truly operating blind. God! "I'm ready to listen now," he said gruffly. "If you still want to tell me." He saw her stiffen, sit up straighter, felt her fingertips dig into the muscles of his chest.

She took a deep, shuddering breath. It was going to be hard, so hard. Some of the things she would tell Mark, she had never told anyone, not even Leo and Maggie. "That night—the night when you told me—made me see how the accident had happened. I was in shock, Mark. When my world was destroyed the first time, I had no center, no direction, nothing to focus on. You became the center of my world for more than a year. You were almost an obsession," she whispered.

"I don't understand."

"You were all I had to hang on to—to blame for what had happened to me. In my mind, you caused it. And my mind conjured you into a shadowy villain that was monstrous enough to be a central character in a Stephen King novel. I was angry, frustrated and miserable. On the surface, I told myself that I accepted what had happened to me. But inside, anger and bitterness were constantly festering. The energies that I had always centered on painting were focused on you."

"You must have really hated me," he said in a low voice.

"I needed you—someone to hate, a target. Because as long as I had you to focus on, I could forget about myself, and what I used to do, but would never do again."

"Paint?"

"Yes. The hate snowballed, until it became larger than life. I lived and breathed it," she admitted, head bent. And then she raised her head slowly. "It kept me alive."

"Dear God! You didn't—"

"No. Oh, no. But everything was so black, there was nothing to fill the empty spaces. Painting has—had been my whole life. I used to paint as long as the inspiration lasted, sometimes far into the night. Leo used to say that one day I'd make a mistake and use paint instead of makeup."

"And you were afraid of the dark."

"Yes."

"And when the monster—the shadow villain—gained substance?"

"I felt . . . betrayed. It hurt."

"You said your world was destroyed twice?"

"The second time was when you told me what had really happened that night. I felt like I was being torn apart. My senses warred with what I had believed for a year. I'd misjudged you terribly. I wasn't ignoring you that night at my house. I was horrified, so ashamed that I couldn't even talk to Leo and Maggie about it until days later. And then I found out from them that you hadn't told me the whole truth, and I felt even worse." She pulled back, removing her hands from him, collapsing against the couch.

"I told you everything, Judith," he protested hoarsely, his fingers digging into her shoulders as he pulled her around to face him. "Did you need Leo and Maggie for confirmation?"

His grasp hurt her tender flesh, but she didn't struggle against it. "I believed you. I just couldn't read between the lines. They told me the next morning."

"I don't know what you're talking about."

"They told me about the cars catching fire. And they told me that you were hurt," she said softly.

He shrugged, then realized that she couldn't see the gesture. "It doesn't matter."

"It *matters*," she said, her voice strained. "Maggie said you had a concussion, and broken ribs and a punctured lung."

"My head was banged up, and I had trouble breathing for a while. It wasn't too bad."

"She said you were bleeding from cuts," Judith pressed, inserting her hands through the cage of his arms, moving them against the crisp cotton of his shirt. "Where else were you hurt?" She felt the movement of his chest against her hands as he heaved a sigh.

"My forehead. It doesn't matter," he said again. "I wasn't exactly handsome before."

"Do you mind if I see for myself, Mark?"

He didn't know what she meant. "How?"

She held out her hands. "I use my fingers to read faces, as well as braille letters. Do you mind?"

Even if he objected, would he be able to say no to her? "If you want to," he said gruffly. When she nodded, he took her right hand and carried it slowly to the left side of his forehead.

Her fingers gently traced the edges of the jaggedly healed wound that had mangled his forehead just above his left eye. What had started out as curiosity yielded to pure feeling. Now she was inundated with waves of empathy; she could feel his pain as her own. "Do you—do you mind if I read the rest of your face?" she asked hesitantly.

Why did it seem so hard to breathe, he wondered. "No. I mean, no, I don't mind."

She raised her left hand until both hands were framing his face. Her sensitive touch registered subtle differences in textures, as her fingers explored the warmth of his skin. She discovered the breadth of his forehead, bushy eyebrows, wide-set eyes, eyelashes that fluttered beneath the lightness of her touch. Her fingertips traced the planes of his face, while the tender flesh of her palms tingled as she felt the bristles of five o'clock shadow and the rugged angularity of cheek and jaw. It was a good face. A strong face. She felt, as well as heard, him swallow as she paused at the sides of his neck.

She started to withdraw her hands, but felt them inch upward, almost of their own accord, into the silky thickness of his hair at the sides of his temples. "Silver," she murmured.

"How did you know?" he asked, startled.

"Feels different." And then, following an impulse she couldn't begin to understand, she used the gentle pressure of her hands to urge his head down, ever lower. Until her mouth found his. And her soul found peace.

His arms went around her, and she lay trustfully against him. Warm. Secure. Complete.

He was intoxicated by the slender weight of her softness against him, her scent filling his nostrils. He bent his head, his mouth brushing the dark silk of her hair.

Neither one of them heard the door open.

"I'm leaving now, Mark. Oh!" Sarah hid a smile at the unfamiliar sight of her usually ultrabusinesslike boss caught in a compromising position.

Embarrassed, Judith pushed at Mark's chest. His arms fell away from her immediately.

Mark cleared his throat. "I'll see you tomorrow, Sarah."

"Don't forget your business meeting this evening."

"Right. Seven o'clock. Thank you, Sarah."

Judith heard the swish of fabric, the closing of the door, and knew that they were alone once more. But the spell of intimacy had been broken. She had accomplished her mission. Her apology had been made and, she hoped, accepted. Now Mark Kendall Leland could be a closed chapter in her life. Somehow the thought lay heavily on her heart. "Thank you for listening to me," she said awkwardly.

Her words, her account of all she had gone through, had torn through him like a knife. And now she was saying "thank you," which sounded suspiciously like the beginning of a goodbye speech. He didn't want that. He looked down at her, saw the trembling of her mouth, the twisting of her clasped hands. Could she be saying one thing and meaning another? There was only one way to find out.

"Do you want this to be goodbye, Judith? Because if you do, I won't push you anymore. I don't have any right, any more than I had the right to intrude at the dance."

"I'm glad you did," she blurted without thinking. And then, more slowly, she added, "Otherwise, I might never have known the truth."

"Thank you," he said humbly.

He got off the couch, then reached down for Judith's hands and helped her to her feet. "I don't know quite how to ask this."

"What's that, Mark?"

"I want to ask you to dinner."

"Is that such a hard question?"

"The last time we tried it, the ending was less than spectacular," he said, laughing wryly. "I didn't know if you'd want to try it again."

She took a deep breath. "Yes. I would."

Hallelujah, he exulted silently. "I can't tonight."

"Your meeting."

"Yeah. My first day back, and I'll be stuck in a smoke-filled room. How about tomorrow night?"

"I'd love to." Then, she sighed, "Oh, no."

"What?"

"I've got to baby-sit Robbie Sullivan. It's Leo and Maggie's anniversary, and I promised, but—"

"Saturday night?" Mark cut in, thinking how adorable she looked when she was flustered.

"Wonderful," she said with relief.

Feeling exuberant, he grasped her hand, carrying it to his mouth.

"What's that for?" she asked a trifle breathlessly.

"I wanted to see if you could read a smile."

5

JUDITH SPENT the better part of Friday working on Personal Touch, paying back some of the hours she'd lost in recent weeks. But by four-thirty she was dressed in jeans and a comfy sweatshirt, her hair drawn back into a French braid, her face free of makeup. All in all, she was perfectly attired for a close encounter with an active seven-year-old like Robbie Sullivan, she told herself as she walked down the front walk and got into a waiting cab. But she would have been less than human if she hadn't wished that her date for the evening would be in his midthirties, rather than seven going on eight.

As she settled back into the seat, she couldn't help remembering the day before, when Mark had called a cab for her. And until it had come, he'd waited with her in the lobby area of his office, telling her of his trip, asking her about Personal Touch. Making her feel comfortable, she realized, a smile of remembrance on her lips. No, more than that, she had to admit. Making her feel wonderful.

For the first time since her aborted date with Mark, if she were to be honest with herself—her spirits were bordering on high. All last evening, even though she'd spent it alone, she'd been aware of a glow, of a feeling of accomplishment. She'd conquered her fears—and his hurt—and had come out whole on the other side. No, it was more than that, she realized, the thought reaching her with acute awareness: the need to soothe Mark's pain had overridden her own fears, not the least of which had been that he would reject her efforts. Reject *her*. She shivered. Suddenly, that was the worst fear of all.

The driver's voice broke into her thoughts as the cab braked to a stop.

"That'll be five dollars, ma'am."

"Give me a minute," she asked as she began the inevitable rummage for her wallet.

"No problem," the man replied. "Take your time."

Compartments. The bag needed compartments, Judith muttered to herself as her fingers sought the feel of the smooth leather of her wallet. Naturally it had sunk to the bottom of the rest of the miscellany she carried with her. Five dollars, the driver had said. She sifted through the bills she carried. To avoid confusion, she folded each kind of denomination a different way when she cashed her checks at the bank. Tens she folded crossways, fives lengthwise. Ones weren't folded at all. She kept larger denominations in their own small labeled plastic envelopes. And the change never presented any problem, since she could tell one coin from another by size and edge. She fished out a five and a one, giving the bills to the driver. "Thanks a lot."

"You need any help, ma'am?"

"Not if we're at 1714 Brandon Avenue."

"You got it, lady."

"Thanks again, then." She slung the bag over her shoulder and got slowly out of the cab. Then she looped the cane over her wrist and walked to the front door, which was opened even before she could get out her key.

Maggie set Judith's bag on the floor, then gave her a hug. "Something's different."

Judith felt the heat rise in her face as she wondered how best to tell Maggie what had happened with Mark. "I . . . feel better."

"That sure tells me a lot," Maggie grumbled.

"Well, I—" But before Judith could say anything else, she was ambushed, engulfed in a waist-crushing hug from Robbie. She scrunched down briefly, wrapping her arms around him in return.

"Hi, Aunt Jude. Watcha bring me?"

"Manners!" Maggie groaned. "Behave yourself, monster."

"Do you want me to carry your stuff upstairs?" Robbie asked.

"Thanks, sport. Stick it on the floor next to the dresser. I'll get what I need from it later."

"Okay."

"How about some tea while we wait for my Prince Charming to get his act together?" Maggie asked with a laugh.

"Love some," Judith replied, making her way into the kitchen.

"Now that my darling son has left the premises, what kind of goodies are in the bag, Aunt Jude?" Maggie asked as she poured tea into mugs.

Judith, who had found a seat by the kitchen table, shifted slightly in her chair. "Oh, you know, nightgown, robe, toothbrush..."

"And?" she prodded, handing Judith a mug of tea.

"And a few jars of finger paints," Judith admitted.

"Oh, no!" Maggie groaned, sinking down into the chair next to Judith.

"Well, you won't let me leave the stuff here. You threatened me with dire consequences."

"The words were 'bodily harm,' if memory serves me correctly. I still can't forget what happened the time Robbie got hold of them."

Judith couldn't forget, either. Two kitchen walls had to be scrubbed, along with the counters, the breakfast table and the floor. "I'll make sure he doesn't, uh, we don't leave any mess," Judith muttered defensively. "It's just that he wants to do the kinds of things we used to do, fooling around with all my art supplies—"

"Hey, I'm just teasing," Maggie cut in, reaching across the table to squeeze Judith's hand. "I'll leave a pile of newspapers on the bottom shelf of the microwave table."

"Thanks, Maggs."

They sat across from each other at the kitchen table, drinking unsweetened tea. Suddenly Maggie broke the silence.

"Did something happen, Jude?" she asked softly.

"Happen?"

"You look—different," Maggie said hesitantly.

"She looks like a teenybopper in that outfit."

"Hello, Leo," Judith replied. "I'm sure you look gorgeous, too."

"I wouldn't trade him," Maggie cut in.

"Glad to hear it, my love."

Judith smiled at their bantering, then got up to rinse out the mugs. She worked easily and quickly in the kitchen whose layout and utensils were nearly as familiar to her as her own, unconsciously tensing as she heard the approach of Leo's footsteps behind her.

She was drying a mug. He took it from her, setting it on the counter, then enveloped her in a hug.

"Good to see you, love."

"You, too, Leo." And then, unable to restrain herself any longer, Judith took a deep breath and said, "I went to see Mark yesterday, even though he didn't want to see me."

"And . . ." Maggie coaxed breathlessly.

"We—we're going out tomorrow night." Suddenly Judith found herself enveloped in a joint hug. "Thanks, both of you," she murmured shakily.

"You did it yourself," Leo said immediately.

"Sure I did. Give me a break!"

"Never mind," Leo said gruffly. "You all set for tonight?"

"You bet," Judith told him, a smile on her face.

"Finger paints," Maggie was heard to mutter darkly.

BEFORE THEY LEFT, Maggie reminded Judith of the burglar-alarm code, the fire extinguisher, pointed out the brailled numbers she had left by the preprogrammed telephone. "The pediatrician, the next door neighbors—"

"The National Guard," Leo put in.

"Shut up, Leo," retorted his wife.

"Dear, we're only going to Washington for the evening. It's not as if Judith has never spent the night here, you know."

But what no one mentioned was that this was the very first time since the accident that she alone would be responsible for Robbie. "Thanks for the numbers, Maggs."

"There's a casserole in the refrigerator."

Judith felt a nudge from Robbie, who was obviously not in the mood for casserole. She nudged him back. "Goodbye, already," Judith hinted broadly, then bent toward the boy. "Later," she whispered.

Later came as soon as the front door closed on Leo and Maggie.

"Can we go to McDonald's, Aunt Jude?"

"Can we make it another time, love?"

"Why? We could get the cab driver to come back."

"Nope, tonight it's Mom's casserole, but we'll figure something out for dessert. We'll do McDonald's another time, okay?"

"I guess so."

She ruffled his hair. "Hey, I'm starved. Why don't you set the table for me while I get things together, huh?" Judith was just about to put the casserole into the oven when the doorbell rang.

"I'll get it," Robbie called.

"*We'll* get it," Judith corrected as she made her way into the living room. There was a peephole in the door, which didn't do her any good, of course. But there was also a chain lock, in addition to the dead bolt.

"I looked through the front window, Aunt Jude. It's a man I never saw before."

He could be selling things, he could be a lost motorist. It made no difference. Whoever he was, she wasn't about to let him in. She opened the door only as far as the chain allowed. "Who is it?"

"Mark."

She froze where she stood, unable to accept the fact that he had come, that he was actually there, separated from her by a mere two inches of wood and flimsy chain. She swayed, grasping the edge of the door frame, grateful for its support. How about that, she mused bewilderedly. Wishes really did come true!

The chain was still in place, the door only partially open. She showed no signs of having heard him. "Judith, may I come in? I think we're starting to cause some gossip out here. The neighbors are getting curious. There are ten to twelve onlookers. The police are setting up a SWAT team command post."

"Oh, brother," Judith groaned as she scrabbled with the chain.

"Hold out your hands. I brought you something."

She did so. What she felt in her hands was certainly no bouquet or box of chocolates. It was a paper bag. Immediately the intoxicating scent of French fries assailed her senses. French fries?

"McDonald's!" Robbie whooped loudly. "Hey, no wonder you didn't want to go out, Aunt Jude. McDonald's came *here*. Neat!"

Her inquisitive fingers immediately identified large servings of fries, beneath which she found a mountain of wrapped burgers. "Why did you bring all this?"

"I remembered that you said Robbie liked Mc-Donald's."

"Boy, do I!" Robbie piped up.

"Thank you, Mark."

"You're welcome."

"Who're you?" Robbie asked the tall man who stood in the doorway.

"Mark Leland."

"I'm Robbie Sullivan."

Mark hunkered down and shook hands with the child. Then he looked up at Judith, who was standing motionless before him. Her chestnut hair was pulled back away from her face, so that she looked about sixteen. He took her hand, as he had Robbie's. He would have liked to do more—to kiss her mouth, as he had yesterday. But when he did that, he didn't want an audience, juvenile or otherwise. "May I stay, Judith?"

"For dinner?"

"Yes."

"Of course, you can. You bought the burgers and fries."

"But I'm uninvited."

"I guess we can manage to put up with you."

"Right," he said, laughing. "You're very gracious."

"I'm hungry, Aunt Jude," Robbie called. "When are you going to heat the food?"

"I'll be right there, Robbie. Get enough plates and napkins for three." Sensing Mark's presence in front of her, she edged around him to close and lock the front door, then headed unerringly for the kitchen.

He followed in her wake, watching as her fingers occasionally brushed against a wall or a piece of furniture. She constantly had to orient herself, he realized. "Do you need a waiter?"

"No. Robbie's taking care of the table. The appliances all have additional controls in braille," she told him automatically. "I can handle things."

And she did. Mark watched silently as she heated up the burgers and fries in the microwave. He forced himself to say nothing when several fries dropped to the floor. He picked them up surreptitiously under the pretext of finding his fallen napkin, then sat back as she took paper cups and filled them with ice cubes. He caught his breath as she opened the refrigerator and took out a two-liter bottle of Coke.

Judith cringed at her own ineptness as she struggled with the huge soft-drink bottle. It was nearly full, and its bullet shape reminded her of a torpedo. She was used to smaller bottles, or twelve-ounce cans. A handle would have helped. Gritting her teeth, she willed her hands to steadiness. She knew how to pour a drink, for God's sake; there was no excuse for an attack of the clumsies. But *there was*, an inner voice taunted as she struggled to pour the stuff into flimsy paper cups that kept wanting to fall down. Mark. All of her careful rehabilitation training and hard-won self-confidence seemed to evaporate in his presence.

Finally he couldn't stand it anymore. He got up, took the bottle from her and poured the drinks.

"Don't do that again," she ordered sharply. "I'm perfectly capable of pouring drinks."

"It looked too large for you to handle. I would have done the same for anybody."

"Sure. Well, I know my limitations, Mark. I don't need you to point them out."

Lord, he'd managed to set her back up again. Would he ever have a chance to redeem himself? "Do you want the drinks taken to the table?"

"You might as well," she grumbled.

"Gee, thanks, 'Aunt Jude.'"

"Be nice, or you don't get dessert," she said, managing to recapture her good humor. Now, if she could only get her racing heart to calm down!

During the meal Judith marveled at the way Mark interacted with Robbie. At no time did he talk down to the child. In fact, she mused, he seemed to be conversant with all of Robbie's interests, which ranged from sports to comic books to the latest in robot battle toys.

Mark divided his attention between Robbie, who was talking a mile a minute, and Judith, who said practically nothing at all.

She only ate half a burger, Mark noticed. Maybe he had made her lose her appetite. As he ate his own cheeseburgers, and listened with half an ear to Robbie's chatter, Mark was struck by Judith's fragility. The mouth that had been so softly tempting against his own the day before was drawn into a tense line.

"You didn't eat very much," he said softly.

She had been too busy worrying about what was going to happen after dinner. There was no way she wanted him hanging around during Robbie's after dinner playtime. Even though she and Mark had settled the past, and there was a possibility of a future, she was still unprepared to expose herself to him. And she was afraid that's exactly what would happen if he stayed much longer. "I didn't have much of an appetite," she said finally.

"Maybe I should license myself as a diet product."

Judith had to smile in spite of herself. "Maybe you should. Who's for ice cream?" she asked as she rose from the table, glad that the meal, which had been so uncomfortably tense for her, was finally drawing to a close. Now all she had to do was get Mark out of the house before Robbie's finger painting started....

"Now, Aunt Jude?" Robbie asked once the table was clean the paper plates and cups safely in the trash.

Oh, Lord. She couldn't face it—not with Mark there. "We'll do it after Mr. Leland leaves," she said, fingers unconsciously shredding the remnants of her napkin.

"Why do I have to leave?" Mark asked.

"Not again," she sighed wearily. "Don't you ever take no for an answer?"

"Not very well, I'm afraid. I just wanted to be here with you. I didn't want to wait until tomorrow night. You don't have to rush through your plans with Robbie on my account."

Honestly, the man had the sensitivity of a grapefruit, she thought, steeling herself against what couldn't possibly be a plaintive note in his voice. The last thing she wanted was for him to watch her make a fool of herself. Whoever heard of a blind artist teaching a seven-year-old the finer points of finger painting? "Never mind, Robbie. We'll do it another time. We can all watch TV tonight."

"I don't want to watch TV," he whined. "And Mom and Dad'll be home tomorrow. Mom hates when I finger paint."

Mark's mouth dropped open. "Finger paint?" he echoed blankly. "You finger paint, Judith?"

Judith could feel Mark staring at her. "Robbie's the painter in the family now. I just help him along. You've heard of finger painting, I suppose?" she asked haughtily.

"I used to do it when I was six or seven."

"A hundred years ago, at least."

"More like twenty-seven or twenty-eight, actually."

"Aunt Jude promised we could do it. You said you'd fix it up with Mom."

"I did, Robbie."

"Then why don't you want to?"

"Yeah, why not?" Mark joined in. "Is there some reason I couldn't stay for the finger painting? Is some secret method being used? Will I upset your concentration?"

That was an understatement, she agreed silently. "I don't want an audience," she muttered.

"Oh, I don't intend to be an onlooker," he said, impulse going into overdrive. "I want to get into the act. If it's all right with you, that is."

Oh, Lord, she groaned inwardly. I don't want you here. I don't need to make a fool out of myself in front of you. She didn't mind working with Robbie. He was family. What was Mark? She didn't want to think about it. "You don't really mean that?" she asked hopefully.

"Sure do," he answered immediately. "Of course, it's been so long since I finger painted that I'm sure I forgot everything I ever knew."

"Aunt Jude could show you, couldn't you?"

She hadn't even agreed that Mark could stay, and now the traitorous child was offering her services as a teacher. "I give up," she muttered. "Robbie, please get my bag from upstairs, and some sheets of paper from the playroom. When you come back, you can cover the table and the floor all around us with the newspapers under the microwave table." When she heard the boy's footsteps fade away, she told Mark, "You can stay, but I doubt if you'll want to paint."

"Why not?"

"Why do you think Maggie has a conniption fit every time Robbie wants to do it? You get dirty from fingertip to elbows, not to mention faces, clothes and the surrounding environment."

"You sound like a weather report, Judith," Mark said as he got to his feet.

She heard him get up, heard his footsteps lead away from the room. Had she won that easily? Why was she somehow disappointed. "You're leaving?" she called.

Don't get your hopes up, lady. "Nope," he called back. "Just taking off my jacket, pocketing my watch and rolling up my shirtsleeves well past my elbows."

"You can't really want to bother..."

"It's no bother. I don't mind getting down and dirty." When it came to Judith Blake, he'd brave a lot more.

"I'm back, Aunt Jude."

Mark sat back in his chair as Robbie brought in a tote bag that was almost bigger than he was, and set it on the floor next to Judith.

"It's on the right side of your chair. I'm going to spread out the newspapers now."

"Thanks, love," Judith replied as she scrabbled in the voluminous bag, her fingers groping awkwardly through a mass of items that seemed to have a life of their own. Finally she found the large Ziploc bag with four jars of paints and several wooden tongue depressors.

"We used to work on all kinds of projects," Robbie said. "I even used to help Aunt Jude in her studio."

"Are the newspapers in place?" Judith asked hurriedly, not wanting to get into any kind of discussion of her late artistic career.

"Going to hide the evidence?" Mark quipped.

"Last time there was a bit of a mess, to say the least. I promised Robbie's mom that there wouldn't be any this time. Right, Rob?"

"Uh, sure."

Mark smothered a laugh as he saw the boy eyeing the jars of red, blue, yellow and green paints with a gleam in his eyes.

"It's not that I don't trust you, Robbie, but I think I'd better double-check."

"The table's fine," Mark assured her.

"Thanks." Without saying anything further, she got off her chair and down to her knees to check under the table.

"I'll check down here," Mark said quickly as he knelt down on the floor underneath his side of the table. "All covered up," he reported dutifully. His fingers accidentally collided with hers as he backed away to get to his feet.

His touch was electric, sending a jolt of sensation all the way up to her wrist. She pulled back immediately, getting out from under the table so quickly that she might have hit her head, or fallen over backwards if Mark hadn't been there to lend a steadying hand.

"Easy. Take it easy," he urged, his tone gentle as he helped her to her feet.

Calm down, Judith told herself as she pawed through the kitchen drawer in search of teaspoons. She took longer than necessary. Let him think that she was too inept to find things; she didn't care. It was more important to gain a measure of control before she sat down across from him again. She put the spoons in her pocket, then took three sheets of glossy paper and wet them down at the sink.

"Everybody take one, and lay on some paint," she said when she brought the papers back to the table and took the spoons out of her pocket.

"What color should I use, Aunt Jude?"

Mark saw her flinch at the boy's question.

"Let's try some wide stripes of blue across the paper."

Judith dipped the side of her right thumb into the paint. Then, using her left hand as a guide, she made three horizontal stripes across the paper. "Spoon," she ordered, holding out her hand.

"Spoon," Mark echoed as he laid the teaspoon into the palm of her waiting hand. And then he watched in amazement as she made white Vs in the strips of color.

"Wow! Great-looking birds, Aunt Jude."

"Sea gulls," Mark murmured under his breath.

"Okay, Robbie, now you try it," Judith urged.

Mark marveled that she didn't mind getting dirty. He saw how she gathered paint on the tongue depressor, layering it onto the paper, then waited until it started to dry before pressing into it with her finger. Then he watched the boy do likewise.

"I guess my hands are pretty dirty, huh?" Judith asked.

"Very," Mark agreed.

She sighed. "Mark, can you get a couple of forks, and the miniature vase that you'll find on the corner of Maggie's desk."

"I think you've lost me, but I'll get the stuff."

Minutes later he marveled at her patience—and her talent—as her fingertips created raindrops, the side of her hand undulated to form seaweed and the heel of her hand rotated to form perfect sea shells. He watched, fascinated, as she showed Robbie how to use a spoon and fork to draw outlines, and the base of the vase to do a kind of intaglio on the thickened paint.

I'll be damned, Mark thought to himself.

"Gee, Aunt Jude, you do better without seeing than I do with my two eyes."

"Thanks, Rob," Judith murmured softly.

Mark felt his throat tighten.

"Aren't you going to paint, too, Mr. Leland?"

"You don't have to," Judith reminded him immediately.

He wasn't about to miss this opportunity. Maybe if he showed Judith his willingness to look a little foolish, she would feel less self-conscious with him. "I don't mind giving it a try, but you should know that I got a 'D' in art. Math was more my strong point."

"Cheer up. I had to take algebra twice. I never knew what 'X' was!" she said, laughing.

His heart quickened at her laughter. "Now what?"

"Now you get 'down and dirty,' like you said you wanted to before we started this little adventure. Just try to do what I just did with Robbie."

Mark took a deep breath, scooped some red paint onto the tongue depressor and went to work. Not satisfied with the streaky results, he added some yellow, then tried some of the techniques he'd seen Judith demonstrate.

"While Mark is working, you tell me about your painting, Robbie."

Mark barely heard what the boy was saying. All he noticed was the tension and strain on Judith's face as the boy told her about the painting she'd helped him create, but couldn't see. The words tore him up. It took such courage to help the boy do what used to be as natural to her as breathing—and now she couldn't even see the results.

"What about you, Mark?"

"Huh?"

"Your painting."

He cleared his throat. "I was trying for a sunrise, I guess." He saw Robbie trying to fight off an attack of the giggles.

"And what *did* you get?" Judith prodded.

"Looks more like a scrambled egg with ketchup on it," Robbie answered, finally losing his fight against the giggles.

"Thanks a lot, kid," Mark said, shaking his head at the mess in front of him.

"Can we try watercolors next time, Aunt Jude?"

"You'll have to get your art teacher to help you with that," she told him, fighting to keep her voice steady. "I can help you with this stuff because I can use my fingers to feel the gooey glop."

"And it sure is gloppy," Mark agreed wryly.

"Right. And speaking of glop, everybody to the kitchen sink to wash off this mess. Luckily it comes off with plain water, Mark. You first, Rob." Judith went next, with Mark bringing up the rear. "All clean?" she asked.

"Except for you, Aunt Jude. You've got paint on your face."

"I'll take care of that," Mark said as he dampened a paper towel and gently wiped a smudge of blue near Judith's mouth. His hand lingered on the smooth skin of her cheek long after the paint was gone.

"Th—thank you," Judith stammered, backing away from him, suddenly shy of his touch. "I'm going to put Robbie to bed."

"And read me a story," the boy said.

"I guess there might be something readable in my bag of tricks," Judith agreed. "You change into your pajamas and I'll be there as soon as I clean up the kitchen."

"If you'll tell me where I can find a large plastic bag, I'll clean up the papers and the rest of the paraphernalia," Mark offered.

"You don't have to."

"I want to," he said quietly. "After all, I helped make the mess. There's no reason why I shouldn't contribute to the cleanup."

She decided to accept his help. It was easier than arguing with him. "There are large plastic bags under the sink. After I read Robbie his story, I'll meet you downstairs."

"What shall I do with the paintings?" Mark asked.

"Robbie's go on a piece of newspaper on the counter, to dry." She didn't need any souvenirs of the evening. "Mine can be pitched."

Mark found the plastic bag and began the task of methodically cleaning up the finger painting residue. But after he'd cleared away the newspapers, mopped up a smudge on one of the kitchen chairs and set Robbie's "works of art" aside, Judith's still remained. He couldn't bring himself to throw it away. Not bothering to analyze his motives, he put the still-damp painting on a piece of newspaper, then very quietly slipped out of the house, laying the painting on the floor in the trunk of his car. It would be the first Judith Blake work that he owned.

When he got back into the house, he intended to go back to the kitchen, but was drawn by Judith's voice. Following that sound, he crept up the stairs and saw her sitting in a low chair in Robbie's room, looking like little more than a child herself. Her fingers whispered across the page as she read a story filled with spaceships and friendly aliens, all the things that were sure to fire a small boy's imagination. As the tale drew to a close, he retreated to the living room, not wanting her to know that he'd been intruding.

The house was quiet. Judith had heard the sound of the front door opening and closing. Mark taking out the trash? And now she tensed, her voice hesitating slightly as she heard him come up the stairs and pause almost within arm's length of Robbie's room. Why, she wondered, as she heard him retrace his steps.

Eventually she sensed that she was alone.

Mark paced back and forth, waiting for Judith to come down.

"Mark?" she called finally, standing poised at the top of the stairs.

"I'm right down here."

His voice was coming from directly below her, where the staircase ended and the entrance hall began. She walked down the stairs, his presence drawing her as if she were falling, and he were gravity itself. "I hope I didn't keep you waiting too long," she said as she reached the first floor.

Any wait is too long, he said to himself, but not to her. "You're worth waiting for."

She felt her cheeks grow warm. "Thank you." And then, because she was too flustered to know what to do next, she asked him if he wanted coffee.

"Uh-uh. Not for me. But if you—"

"No. I mean—"

"I'm making you nervous, aren't I?" he asked softly.

She took a deep breath. "I guess I'm making myself nervous. I'm not dressed for a date."

"Hey, I'm not a date. I'm just an uninvited guest, remember?" Then, he continued, "Do you mind if we just sit and talk for a while?"

"No, I don't mind," she said, walking beside him.

"I'm glad you're letting me stay, darlin'."

She stopped in her tracks, her mind whirling as past and present flowed together in a seamless current. "Now I understand," she murmured.

"What's that?" he asked, capturing her hand and leading her to the corner of the many-sectioned sofa. He slid his arm behind her slender waist as she sat down beside him.

"Flashbacks, Mark."

"I don't understand."

"You told me you get nightmares. I get flashbacks. I never knew what they were, what they meant. I never even told anyone. I really didn't want to be poked and prodded anymore."

"What kind of flashbacks, Judith?"

"Just snatches of things. A faint Southern drawl, for one."

"I lived in Texas for five years. I guess it rubbed off on me. What else?"

She smiled. "Being called *darlin'*."

"A term of endearment." His arm tightened slightly around her.

She laughed softly. "And then there was a certain scent. I smelled it then, and again the night of the dance. And every other time you've been near me. I always associate it with you." She would know him anywhere, any time.

"Sandalwood. It's just the kind of soap I use."

Her smile faded as she gingerly searched memories long buried. You clung to me, Mark had said that night at her house. She remembered strong arms around her, arms that had made her feel safe and secure, despite everything. "That night—the night of the accident—I remember being held," she whispered.

She felt him lean toward her, sensed the heat of his body seeking her own inner warmth. She didn't resist, giving herself over to the welter of feelings that poured over her.

He took her in his arms, as he had long ago. His mouth found hers, his tongue tracing the outline of her lips, which opened as she took a deep breath. Her nearness set his heart racing, very nearly eclipsing the voice of reason that told him it was too soon. His erratic heartbeat threatened to suffocate him. His blood surged painfully, making his groin ache. But he forced himself to hold back, not wanting to frighten her with the depth of his need. The tentative movement of his mouth on hers was a ballet of tenderness.

Judith waited for Mark to deepen the kiss, wondering why it didn't happen. And then, through the fog of sensuality that seemed to envelop them both, she became aware of the tension in him. She didn't need sight to be aware of his quickened breathing, the thunder of his heart against her breast. She reached out, placing her hands on his shoulders, and felt him tremble beneath her touch. Somehow, she knew without words that despite his greater masculine strength, Mark, too, had doubts, needed reassurance.

Her hands inched upward, tangling in the soft, thick hair at the base of his neck. Very gently she urged his head downward, her lips parting on a soundless plea.

For an instant he froze, utterly still beneath her touch. Then he breathed her name before fusing his mouth to hers, his tongue finding entrance to a moist, honeyed sweetness he had barely imagined.

How much time passed, Judith didn't know. The kiss seemed to go on and on, changing, evolving, plumbing the depths of her emotions. And finally, when air became a necessity, she breathed. By the time she took her next breath, every nerve was sensitized. Her arms were wrapped around Mark, her aching breasts crushed against the crisp cotton of his shirt as he lay above her. And the hard ridge of his masculinity pressed into the cradle of her feminine warmth.

With each uneven breath he took, Mark felt Judith's hardened nipples against his chest. He shifted slightly, one arm braced to support his weight above her. With his other hand, he traced the perfection of her form, shaping the curves of her tautened breasts, each touch a lingering caress. And all the while he felt an electric surge of pure joy as her fingers dug relentlessly into the straining muscles of his back, urging him even closer to her.

She wanted him! His emotions wavered between heartfelt thanks and disbelief. And he wanted *her*—had wanted and waited . . . so long. This time, he thought, there was no one to take her away from him. No paramedics, no well-meaning secretary reminding him of a business meeting. . . .

"Aunt Jude!"

"Damn!" Mark hissed, his breath coming in gasps.

Robbie's plaintive wail effectively poured cold water on the fragile bonds of intimacy.

"My thoughts exactly." She sighed, letting her head sink back against the cushions. "That's what happens when you crash somebody else's party."

Using all the control at his command, Mark eased himself reluctantly and painfully away from Judith. "You—go on up and see what he wants. I'll wait for you."

Surely he could see that it would never work—that she shouldn't have let things get carried away. . . . "Mark."

"I'll wait to say good night."

"Oh. Right."

Rising to her feet more than a little unsteadily, Judith went to find out what Robbie wanted. It turned out to be a prosaic drink of water. Maybe it was better this way, she tried to tell herself as she tucked the child back into bed and pressed a kiss to his forehead. Maybe things were moving too fast, and she wouldn't be able to handle it.

Once more, Mark waited for Judith at the bottom of the stairs. This time, jacket in hand. "About tomorrow, Judith?"

Did he want to cancel? Had her "artistic performance" turned him off? Maybe he regretted suggesting the dinner date and was looking for a way out. "What about it?" she asked breathlessly. Once more, she found herself in his arms; she could sense that his mouth was poised just above her own.

"Is it going to be just the two of us?"

She smothered a sound that was caught somewhere between a laugh and a sigh of relief. "As far as I know."

"Thank you," he murmured fervently, the melding of his mouth with hers underlining his words.

When his mouth left hers, Judith felt lost, bereft. His hoarsely spoken good-night was a shock to her system.

"Walk me to the door?"

"Okay."

"If I don't leave now," he said, taking a breath, "I'll never be able to. Tomorrow night at seven?"

"Yes."

"Sleep well."

"I'll—work on it."

"Damn," he muttered, bending his head so he could press one more quick, hard kiss to her mouth. Then he gave her braid a gentle tug. "Lock up behind me."

"Right." The door was no problem, she brooded as she worked the lock and chain, and set the burglar alarm. The problem was her heart.

She was very much afraid that it had already been stolen.

6

"HOLD OUT YOUR hands, Judith."

Knowing Mark Leland was turning out to be a real adventure, Judith mused in silent wonder. All day long she'd been living on nerves, waiting for seven o'clock—and Mark—to arrive. And now that she'd opened the door for him, he was just standing there, not moving. She knew something was . . . different.

The sandalwood scent she'd come to expect was obscured by an odd mixture of fragrances. He made no move to come in. His silence wasn't doing a lot for her rather fragile self-confidence. And then there was that curious rustling sound. "Is something—wrong?" she asked hesitantly.

For a long moment he'd been so captivated by her utter loveliness that he'd forgotten to speak. Now, as he saw the confusion on her face and the stiffness of her posture, he was mentally kicking himself. "Hello, Judith. Of course nothing's wrong. Just hold out your hands."

"Burgers and fries?" she quipped, her nervousness fading as she remembered the night before.

"Not hardly," he replied with a laugh. "I'm going to feed you, but I doubt if you'll find this edible. Now, hold out your hands." He carefully placed his offering in her outstretched arms.

One moment, her arms had been empty. Now they were filled with food—this time for the senses: flowers! "Oh,

Mark!" Judith cried, burying her nose in the exquisite array of scents. "How did you know I love flowers?"

"Lucky guess." It wasn't, not really. He'd noticed how oriented she was to touch, taste, smell and hearing.

"I'll just put them in water," she said, intending to head for the kitchen where she knew she would find a vase. And then she stopped, turned back, stood on tiptoe and pressed a fleeting kiss to his mouth. "I'll be back."

He wanted to go after her. The kiss was a mere hors d'oeuvre, and he was hungry for more. But he held back, jamming his hands into his pockets.

"There," she said as she returned to the living room and set the vase on the coffee table. "How do they look?"

"Gorgeous." And he wasn't referring just to the flowers. He feasted his eyes on the plum-colored jumpsuit that outlined her slender form to perfection. A pulse beat in her throat, and her breasts pressed against the soft fabric with every breath she took. More than anything, he wished he could forget about going out for dinner and stay here with Judith, food or not. But he couldn't do that; he'd promised to take her out to dinner. And he'd vowed to himself that this evening was damn well going to make up for the earlier disaster. He cleared his throat. "Are you ready?"

"I'll just get my jacket."

"I'll get it," he said, having noticed it on the back of the sofa.

All too aware of Mark, Judith shivered at the pressure of his hands on her shoulders.

He backed off instantly. "What's wrong? I know something is." He swallowed hard. "Are you having doubts about going out with me tonight?"

"I know it's stupid, but I guess I—I'm nervous." She took a deep breath. "Well, now you know," she said, her hands clasped tightly in front of her.

Mark came forward, wanting nothing more than to take her into his arms for reassurance, but knowing instinctively that now was not the time. Instead, he covered both of her hands with his own, saying the first thing that came into his mind. "You're not the only one, lady."

She cocked her head to the side. "*You* are?"

"'Fraid so," he admitted, using his grasp on her hands to gently draw her toward him. "Like I said in my office, our first date was less than spectacular. I've been making up lists of restaurants, places you might like to go—" His breath caught in his throat at the way the frown disappeared from her face, to be replaced by a smile that kindled fires deep inside his body.

"Oh, Mark," she murmured, inexpressibly touched that she hadn't been the only one to worry. "I don't care where we go. Anywhere is fine with me."

His heart leaped, then settled down into a seminormal rhythm. "I hope you're hungry."

She took a deep breath. "Starving."

"Do you like seafood?"

"Love it," she agreed instantly.

"We'll be going to a rather unique place," he said. And it couldn't be more different from the elegantly intimate restaurant he'd taken her to the first time, he added silently.

He took her to Phillips, a boisterous restaurant at Harbor Place, where they sat on wrought-iron chairs and worked their way through highly seasoned shrimp and crab legs, washing it all down with icy cold beer.

Occasionally each had to shout to be heard above the honky-tonk music that was played in the background on a rinky-dink piano. Throughout the meal she was all too aware of his nearness, and of the warm breath she felt against her face whenever he had to lean close to speak to her over the volume of the music.

"Dessert?" he asked when mounds of seafood had given way to piles of shells. He watched, fascinated, as her tongue flicked out to lick traces of spice from her lips.

"I'm stuffed," Judith said finally, leaning back with a sigh of repletion. "What I really need is a four- or five-mile walk to work off all of this wonderful food."

"No sooner said than done," Mark said as he called for the check.

They walked hand in hand around the Inner Harbor. Along the way they listened to the gulls, sniffed the smell of cinnamon that wafted out of the McCormick Spice Company, enjoyed the feel of soft breezes over the water. And through it all, as Mark described the night in terms of the visual, Judith painted word pictures using the senses at her disposal.

And when they had come full circle, back to the glass-enclosed pavilion that housed the restaurant, Mark asked Judith where she wanted to go next.

She took a deep breath. "Once upon a time, I promised you some coffee and brandy. I'd like to make good on the offer."

Within the hour they were back at Judith's house.

While Judith fixed coffee, Mark took off his jacket and tie, then had his first real chance to look around, to examine her surroundings. Her home was very neat, methodical, orderly. He scanned the furnishings, wondering what made the place look so different, so unique. And then he realized that almost everything was oriented to the senses, especially touch.

The carpeting was deeply piled, the sofa covered in a velvety textured fabric. Overstuffed throw pillows in different shapes and sizes were stacked nearby, and covered in fabrics where the design was virtually three-dimensional. And surprisingly—or perhaps not, if the place had been decorated before the accident—there was a wonderful sense of color. There was also a sophisticated entertainment center, and a rather eclectic selection of compact discs, audio and videocassettes, and a great many oversize volumes, which he presumed to be in braille.

He followed the smell of brewing coffee into the kitchen, watching as she assembled everything on a tray with her usual economy of motion. Instinct made him want to pick up the tray and carry it into the living room for her. Then he remembered what had happened at the Sullivans' when he had commandeered the mammoth bottle of soft drink. "May I take that in for you?" he asked, hoping the request sounded casual and matter-of-fact.

He wasn't blatantly taking over, as he had last night, Judith realized, as pleased as if he'd given her a gift. He wasn't thumbing his nose at her hard-won independence. "Yes. Thank you."

Mark set the tray on the coffee table, then sat down next to Judith on the deeply cushioned sofa.

When Judith handed him a cup, Mark dutifully took a sip, not caring how hot it was. Usually he enjoyed good coffee. But tonight it might as well have been Mississippi mud for all the enjoyment he was deriving from it. He had to smother a groan when she asked him if he wanted a second cup. "I'm fine," he murmured.

"Would you like the brandy now, then? There's a liquor cabinet—" She heard him take a breath.

"What I really want..."

"Yes?" she asked, feeling as if she were poised at the brink of an abyss.

The waiting silence had a life of its own.

"You know what I'd really like, Judith?"

"No," she whispered. "W-what would you like?"

"I'd like to be able to turn the clock back about twenty-four hours."

"You want another finger-painting lesson?" she gasped, a gurgle of laughter bubbling up in her throat.

"No," he laughed softly, one long finger gently tracing the contour of her tempting mouth. "Although it was very, uh, enlightening." His hand reached out to shape the delicate line of her jaw. "I can't stop thinking about what happened after that—after you put Robbie to bed."

She quivered at his touch. "I can't stop thinking about it, either."

He touched his mouth to hers, tasted the bittersweetness of coffee on her lips, felt the edge of her teeth with his tongue. Sipping. Drowning.

His lips caressed, soothed, gentled. He lured, coaxed, seeking entrance, not intruding.

Her lips opened beneath his unspoken request, bidding him welcome. She tasted essence of coffee; it should have been bitter. It was dark and sweet.

There was no need for words. Mark's hand slid under Judith's hair, capturing the nape of her neck.

She swallowed, arching toward him, her own hand reaching out and finding the hardness of his shoulder beneath the crisp fabric of his shirt.

At the touch of her hand, he felt something give way inside—something that had been hard, solid and impenetrable. He gathered her into his arms, for the first time yielding to feelings that had been dammed up too long. It was wonderful to hold her—just that—to feel her in his arms and know that the ax wasn't going to fall, that he was going to be discovered, that she would walk away from the person he really was.

Free, that's how she felt; finally free. Even though she was clasped tightly in his arms, her breasts crushed against the hardness of his chest, she didn't feel constrained. She was holding him just as tightly, striving to get even closer, wanting to become a part of him.

He backed away slightly, breathing hard.

Her hands moved in tandem, one at his nape, the other exploring the well-developed muscles clearly evident through the thin fabric of his long-sleeved shirt.

He pressed his mouth to her throat, felt her swallow, her breath catch. So many times during the evening his gaze had focused on her jumpsuit, and the way the opening of the collar ended tantalizingly close to the swell of her breasts.

She felt his mouth at her throat, then felt his lips moving lower, outlining the opening of her collar. His hand followed the movement of his mouth, his fingers barely grazing her flesh, yet arousing her almost unbearably.

Then his hand moved lower, gently shaping the fullness of her breast. He heard her quick intake of breath, saw the pulse of life fluttering in her throat. He felt the mound of softness tauten, pulsating with each reverent touch of his hand.

His touch rendered her virtually mindless, reduced to a creature of feeling, connected to him by an unbreakable force. She only knew that she had to get closer to him, nearer to the warmth that radiated from him like a furnace.

Her hands found the open-necked collar of his shirt, her fingers discovered the curly hair that crowded into the hollow at the base of his throat. Her palms pressed against the hardness of his chest, her fingers restlessly shifting as she felt his hand gently kneading her breast. She could feel his rigid arousal pressing against the vulnerable junction of her legs, she could hear his erratic breathing. And she exulted in the knowledge that she wasn't the only one affected by the explosive forces of passion.

She felt his hand on the tab of her zipper.

He said one word—her name.

She found herself blazing, her skin on fire, her mind whirling. For the first time she truly understood the term "slow motion."

Her breathing grew erratic at the sensual movement engendered by the parting of the fabric, the feel of air against her skin, the constantly gentle abrasion as his mouth grazed her tender flesh. His lips lingered at the gentle mounds of her breasts, swelling with each unsteady breath she took. Her delicately lacy bra had a front clasp. He released it. The zipper inched farther down, exposing the smooth skin of her midriff and the flatness of her belly to his touch.

She had no thought of stopping him, fearing nothing but the intensity of her own feelings, afraid only of wanting him too much. It was unlike anything she'd ever felt before. She shifted under his tender assault as his hand ventured lower and she arched to meet his touch.

He tensed, straining with the effort to retain control—not to rush her.

She felt his slightly unsteady hand on her hair. Then, to her dismay, Judith could feel Mark's tense withdrawal. Dazed, she fought back tears of frustration. And before she could help herself, she reached out to stop him. "Don't go," she whispered after a beat of stillness.

He went still, dropping his head to her forehead. "Believe me," he groaned, "I'm not going anywhere!" He pulled her into his arms, giving her a brief, tight hug. Then he eased away from her.

"What's wrong?"

"Nothing, darlin'," he murmured as he grasped her hand and gently pulled her to her feet. "I want to see you. All of you."

She began to shrug out of her jumpsuit but found his hands on her shoulders, stilling her movements.

"Let me, Judith. Please."

Her zipper was already down. She stood motionless, swallowing dryly as she felt his hands ease the rest of the material away from her. A kiss followed each touch as his fingers and his mouth worked in tandem. Finally fabric whispered past the slim lines of her body. The unclasped bra and lacy panties followed.

"So lovely," he breathed, hypnotized by the sight before him.

She stepped out of the pool of clothes at her feet and was immediately drawn into his embrace, the fabric of his clothing an erotic contrast against her heated skin. His mouth fused to hers, one hand sought her breast and the living force of his desire pressed urgently against her, as if seeking entrance.

She was so wrapped up in her churning emotions and in the luxury of his embrace that when he moved away from her, she shivered as if she'd been plunged into icy water.

"You're cold," he murmured, picking up the afghan that was folded along the back of the sofa, tenderly draping its soft folds around her.

I couldn't be warmer, she could have told him, but refrained, loath to spoil the sweetness of his gesture. Then she heard sounds which she instinctively identified—the rustle of Mark's clothes—and tried to imagine what he looked like. "You're getting undressed," she blurted, annoyed at the warmth that she knew must be rising in her face.

He paused as he finished unbuttoning his shirt. She was blushing, looking for all the world as if she were embarrassed to see him take off his clothes. But of course that couldn't be, Mark knew, the thought punctuated by an all too familiar stab of grief. "Am I making you uncomfortable?" he asked, pausing in the act of unbuttoning his shirt.

She shook her head slowly.

"It's okay to touch, you know," he murmured softly.

She had danced with him. He had held her in his arms. She had felt that symmetrical hardness of muscle and bone concealed beneath the camouflaging layers of fabric. What would he be like when the movements stopped? Her skin was bared to his sight. She quivered in anticipation of the moment when her fingers would be able to learn the subtle nuances of muscle, bone and flesh that made this man. "I want to . . ."

"I'm right in front of you, Judith."

She extended her hand, her very core aching with the need to touch him as he had touched her. As iron filings to a magnet, her fingers were drawn to his chest, directly over his rocketing heart. Her sensitive palm faithfully reported the different sensations. Smooth, silky. Rough, hard. Tempered strength. Reassuring. Solid. The hair on his chest was soft. Her hands traveled to his waist, then trembled. "I've never done this before."

He swallowed hard. "In—the dark?"

She nodded, her lip caught between her teeth as she fumbled with the buttons of his shirt.

He reached down to still her hands. "Think of it as an adventure. Kind of like blazing a trail."

She let her head fall forward, nuzzling her cheek against the hardness of his chest. "It's not only that. I'm . . . out of practice. Greg didn't—he wasn't crazy about touching or being touched. The preliminaries were never important to him, as they were to me," she said, her voice dropping to a whisper. And she'd had more closeness tonight and last night with Mark than in her whole time with Greg.

Damn the bastard, Mark swore inwardly. He winced at her story, cursing the other man for warping her ideas about sex. And yet, if Greg Hollins hadn't been a selfish louse... Mark didn't bother to complete the thought. "Well, darlin', touching, being touched, holding—they're all important to me. Even if we didn't go any further, if we did nothing more than hold each other," he said, one hand trembling slightly as he stroked her hair, "this would already be the best night of my life."

"Oh, Mark," she murmured, her lips stringing a chain of kisses at the base of his neck. Her fingers were surer now, hardly trembling at all as she unbuttoned his shirt and experienced the joy of learning his body for the first time. Her fingers sifted through the silky thickness of his hair; it felt good to the touch. She lowered her head, using her tongue like a brush—his hair had the softness of sable.

Unbidden, her mind flashed back to life-studies classes, when she'd had to draw nude models. Now, with her mouth and hands on his body, it was like bringing a canvas to life. Only this was no two-dimensional figure to be immortalized by brush and palette. Here was a living, breathing man whose every muscle and sinew was hers to discover and learn, and burn into memory.

It was exquisite torture for Mark to feel Judith's mouth and hands on him and do nothing but watch her fingers and lips at work. But even though he was impatient to make love to her, he restrained himself, deriving an immense satisfaction from the light touch of her hands, and then her lips, on his bare skin—as if she was marking the place, familiarizing herself with him. Her touch stimulated him unbearably, pushing his control to the limit. And by the time she reached his belt buckle, he was gritting his teeth with the effort not to simply throw her down on the sofa and make love to her then and there.

"Judith," he gasped, his constricted arousal forcing the blood to pound rhythmically through his veins until he thought he would shatter. "I want you so badly. If you go on this way, I won't be able to wait. I'll be taking you right here."

"You don't have to wait," she said instantly, her hand sliding under his to mold the pulsating shape of his desire.

A current of aching need coursed through him, his fingers infuriatingly clumsy as he made short work of the rest of his clothes. One thing he made sure to remember was the little foil packet that was in the pocket of his slacks.

She listened to the click of metal on metal, the rasp of the zipper, the soft grunts that emanated from him. Then, with uncanny accuracy, she reached for his hand. Her mind seemed to home in on him, have him programmed into her grid of awareness. She smiled as she felt his fingers wrap around hers, then tugged at his hand, sensing somehow that *he* needed reassurance.

He followed without question, taking her in his arms once more, molding her against him, marveling at the way her body fit his. "Judith," he whispered, his mouth against her ear.

"I want you, Mark." She laid her head on his chest, then put her arms around his neck and kissed him, her tongue delivering a message that could not be mistaken. Branding. Leaving no doubt. "I want you. . . ."

He flicked a glance at the lamps that were lit around the room. "Do you mind if I leave the lights on?"

She swallowed. "I hadn't thought about it, I guess. Why?"

"I want to see you, all of you. But I can turn them off, if you want. I don't want to have an unfair advantage," he murmured.

"Oh, I intend to take advantage of you, too."

He let out a burst of laughter, kissing her hard on the lips.

She put her arms around his neck, drawing him down to her.

He caught her close. Closer. Allowed his mouth to surrender to the lure of her parted lips beneath his. Pressing her down into the yielding cushions of the sofa, he lost all track of time, barely retaining enough presence of mind to prepare himself.

For the first time in her life, Judith felt totally unrestrained, returning kiss for kiss, touch for touch. And when his fingers gently probed the moist curls that concealed her femininity, her legs parted for him, her hand reaching out with uncanny accuracy to find him, to guide him to the emptiness that only he could fill.

What followed was exquisitely tender.

"It's been a long time for you, hasn't it, Judith?" Mark asked, panting slightly as he held himself severely in check.

She could feel herself blushing. "Yes."

"Trust me," he urged, his words punctuated by a kiss she felt to the depths of her soul. "I won't hurt you."

"I know you won't."

Mark was so careful, as if she were breakable. No one had ever treated her that way. Even the slightest movement he made became a caress that seemed designed to further her pleasure. His hand brushing the hair back from her forehead caused her to shiver in anticipation. His mouth fused with hers in a union that was a presage of things to come. The powerful male body poised just above her seemed too far away. Close. She wanted him to become part of her. "Mark. *Please*."

Her breath came in staccato pants as he entered her slowly, easing carefully into her. Pressure built within her, became a part of her, until the only thing she knew was the ache of wanting, the need to welcome him into the depth of her, the yearning for completion a tender pain that she willingly suffered.

"I can't—Mark—"

"It's all right, darlin'," he urged, nearly breathless with the way she had welcomed him into the depths of her tight sheath. "You *can*. Let go." He lowered his head, his mouth and tongue suckling first one breast, then the other. "I'll keep you safe."

Safe. Her mind barely recognized the word as she was caught up in a darkness blacker than any she had ever known. And then shattered into a million pieces as the darkness splintered into an explosion of sensuality—with Mark as its focus.

As never before in her life, Judith experienced the purity of ecstasy. Gradually she came back to awareness. Mark was with her, *within* her, his hardness still one with her inner warmth. "Mark, you didn't . . ."

"This was for you, darlin'."

She felt his tension, his control, the stiffness of him, the puffs of air on her sweat-dampened skin as he spoke. She tunneled her fingers into the damp hair at the nape of his neck, her hips rocking in sensual invitation. "Mark, I don't want to be alone. I want you with me."

Mark gasped at the delicious friction that she had initiated, keeping such an iron grip on his control that he was shaking with the effort of holding back. Finally his instincts overrode his conscious mind as he dove into her with ever-deeper strokes. And felt himself splintered by spikes of pleasure that bordered on pain....

"I'm too heavy," she heard a masculine voice say aeons later. For an answer, she held him close to her, her hands clasped in the sweat-moist hollow at the small of his back.

His heartbeat leapt at her gesture. Still linked to her in the most intimate of ways, he carefully shifted his weight, turning so that she was facing him, her back to the couch. His arms were around her, tucking her securely against him. The last words in his mind before he crossed the threshold of sleep were: never let me go....

She had never made love in the dark before—not the dark of blindness. Before this evening, she had even dreaded it. But now she knew that it wasn't being sighted that made the difference. It was the man who had made love to her—and with such exquisite tenderness that the tears had come to her eyes.

She could barely think, let alone speak. But the words had to be said. The man blanketing her with his warmth had a right to hear them. "You were right, Mark."

"Hmm?" he asked sleepily.

"I'm lucky I didn't marry Greg."

USUALLY THE BRIGHT SUN woke Mark; this time, it was the cold that penetrated the lightweight afghan that didn't quite provide enough cover for either Judith or himself. He brushed his fingers lightly against her cheek; her skin was cold. He looked down at her, at the way she lay curved seductively against his body. The last thing in the world he wanted to do was move. Smothering a sigh, he very carefully slid out from under the afghan.

Judith shivered at the sudden absence of Mark's warmth. "What is it?" she mumbled in a sleep-laden voice.

"Shh. It's all right. I'm going to take you upstairs."

"Why?" She wanted only for him to wrap her once more in the cocoon of his warmth.

He kissed her lightly on the nose, which was cold to the touch. "Because it's getting to be like the North Pole down here, and if we don't do something—"

"We're going to have icicles hanging from some rather interesting places," she said, laughing softly.

"Oh, Judith, you are a delight." He lifted her, afghan and all, into his arms.

"I can walk, you know. I seem to remember saying that to you in your office."

"I know, love," he replied, ignoring her. "But it's much more romantic this way, don't you think?"

"Who am I to knock romance?" she complained in mock resignation as she wrapped her arms around his neck.

Even half-asleep, Judith automatically noted the eleven steps to the second floor—she had counted them often enough. Her heart beat faster with each step Mark took, then nearly ground to a halt as he paused by the first door.

Somehow, she had known he would. "Not—that room," she said, her fingers unconsciously embedding themselves in the curve of his neck. "My room is across the hall."

"How did you know where I stopped?" he asked, trying not to flinch at the bite of her nails in his flesh, and at the same time, noting how she had tensed in his arms.

"I count steps," she said tersely.

What was behind that closed door, he wondered, remembering her reaction. He shook his head. Whatever it was, it was her own business, he told himself as he walked through the doorway she had indicated. Flipping back the slick satin comforter, he laid her gently on the bed, then slid in beside her. In moments they were buried under mounds of downy softness, but he could tell that she was no more relaxed than when she had frozen in his arms moments earlier.

It didn't matter, he told himself. The important thing was that she trusted him enough to make love with him. Maybe someday she would trust him enough to tell him what lay behind the door of the room she didn't want him to see.

She lay stiffly beside him, saying nothing, her mind on her overreactive behavior moments earlier. Not only had she ordered him around, treating him with a curtness he didn't deserve, she had physically hurt him. She had felt him flinch. Taut with nervousness, she inched toward him, focusing on the heat of his body. Gritting her teeth, she felt his waiting stillness as she placed her fingers to the left side of his neck over the region scored by her nails.

"I'm sorry, Mark, for what happened earlier. I shouldn't have snapped at you."

"Judith—"

"And I hurt you."

"And now you're going to kiss it all better, aren't you?"

Nonplussed because she had expected anger instead of undemanding acceptance, she blurted, "Is that what you want?"

"Try it and see," he urged softly.

She was to the right of him. The nail gouges were on the left side of his neck. She started to get out of the bed.

"Going somewhere?" Mark asked, amused at her machinations.

"I—" She cleared her throat, but it didn't dispel the huskiness in her voice. "The damage is on the other side."

"Didn't you ever hear that the shortest distance between two points is a straight line?"

"What does that have to do with—"

"Just bear with me, darlin'."

Before she had time to draw another breath, he had taken her in his arms, then eased her gently on top of him. Shyness warred with excitement as she grasped his shoulders for support; she had never been in that position before. Her breasts nestled in the forest of hair that covered his muscular chest; her belly was seared by the heat of his pulsating masculinity.

She felt him shiver as she explored the area of his neck and shoulders in search of what she had done. To her chagrin, she found four deep gouges. She stroked the place with her fingertips, then slid up his body until she could repeat the movement with her mouth, as if to draw out the pain.

When she tried to apologize, to explain, he silenced her with his mouth, the rapier thrust of his tongue plunging into the dark cavern framed by her soft lips. And as if to underline his intent, the pulsating thrust of his masculine heat surged against the yearning emptiness in her belly.

The friction of her body moving over his was more than either of them could bear. There was only one way to quench the fires that burned so brightly. He lifted her carefully over him, heard her soft gasp as he pressed for entrance. She arched, moving to accommodate him, her hands anchored in the thickness of his hair, her tongue delving into the recesses of his mouth as he entered her.

Their lovemaking was fast and furious, as he plumbed depths she never knew she had, taking her farther than she had ever been before. And he was with her all the way to the shattering explosion that blotted out everything else in the universe.

THE BRIGHT MORNING LIGHT woke him up. He looked down with great tenderness at the woman curled seductively into his side, her hand over his heart as if she were taking possession. She had. She owned it. He had given her the key. If he had his way, she would stay there always. The question was, did *she* want it?

Only time would tell, Mark acknowledged as he stole silently from the bed.

After shaving with Judith's razor he showered in the guest bathroom so as not to wake her. In deference to her blissful state of unconsciousness, he had refrained from his usual off-key concert, virtuously congratulating himself on his restraint. After cleaning up he went in search of yesterday's clothes, which he found in a wrinkled heap in the living room. Judith's, he deposited on the chair in her bedroom. His, he put on, minus jacket and tie.

Then Mark walked down the second floor hall as he prepared to leave the house. He had plans for this very special Sunday, and he wanted them carried out before Judith woke up.

But something stopped him in his tracks as he walked past the room with the closed door. His common sense told him to keep on walking. But some deep-seated impulse attracted him like a magnet. Simple curiosity, a part of him said. Invasion of privacy, another voice taunted. Drawn toward the door, he curled his palm around the knob, opened it—and absorbed what felt like a direct blow to the heart.

She hadn't wanted him to see the room; he wished from the depth of his being that he hadn't. Words tumbled end over end in his mind as his gaze was trapped by what he saw: a doorway to hell. Pandora's box.

He saw a blindingly bright room, with large, curtainless windows. If only he had left well enough alone—or bad enough as it was. His roving gaze cataloged easels. A massive work table. Empty canvases stacked against a wall. Half-done sketches. What looked to be gallons of paint. Oversize brushes.

He leaned against the door, his mind struggling to take it all in. This room had been the cradle of her creativity, the place where she'd poured her heart and soul onto canvas, captured imagination in two dimensions.

Over everything was a visible layer of dust. And why not, he ground out bitterly as he turned and left, shutting the doorway to hell behind him. The room was Judith's studio. No one had used it in more than a year. The words echoed in his head as he picked up her key ring from the entrance-hall table and left the house.

JUDITH WOKE UP as she always did—alone. No, that wasn't right, she told herself. She wasn't alone. Not today, not *this* morning. Mark was there. All she had to do was find him.

She called his name; there was no answer. She tried searching in both of the bathrooms, the living room. Silence was the house's only other occupant. Telling herself that it didn't matter, she went outside to sample the morning air. But what she was really doing was looking for Mark's car, which had been parked in the driveway when he'd brought her home last night. The car was gone.

"*Damn him,*" she grated, furious at Mark because he'd left—and at herself, because she was stupid enough to care. Even Greg had had the good manners to say goodbye. Mark Leland was a new kind of lowlife. After showering, she put on a pot of coffee, automatically pouring herself a cup when the timer went off. But she let it get cold, not bothering to drink any of the fragrant brew. She had no desire to eat, either.

Why? she asked herself morosely. Why had he done all that pursuing, just to walk out without even saying goodbye? And she'd been easy, giving him just what he wanted, as if she were a cheap whore in a motel. Lost in thought, her heart shifted into overdrive when she heard the front door open. "Who's there?" she managed.

"It's me," Mark called out, sniffing appreciatively as he carried the results of his Sunday-morning shopping expedition into the kitchen, setting things down on the counter.

Her shoulders sagged in relief, then she stiffened at his casual entrance, as if it were normal for him to wander in and out of her house at will every day in the week.

"Oh, good, you made coffee."

When she didn't say anything, Mark knew something was wrong. When he came near her, she was stiff and unapproachable. And when he put his arms around her, intending to give her a hug, she pulled back, shrugging off his touch. "What's wrong?"

She shook her head.

"Talk to me," he insisted quietly.

She bit her lip, then decided there was no point in concealing her thoughts from him. "I—I wasn't expecting you back."

Pause. "Damn," he muttered. "I should have known. I wanted to bring you something special for breakfast. You were asleep. I didn't want to wake you up, and I didn't know how to leave you a note."

Now it was her turn to utter a curse. "I should have shown you. I have a cassette player, and a braille notetaker, and—"

"Hey, it's no big deal."

She took a deep breath. "Let's start again, huh?"

"Okay by me," Mark agreed, instantly drawing her into his arms and kissing her hungrily. To his great delight, he felt her arms lock around the back of his waist, and her mouth fuse to his.

"Who wants breakfast anyway?" he gasped when air finally became a necessity.

Her grin was enough to light up a dark room. "I do. What did you bring me?"

"How do you know I brought you anything?" he teased.

"I heard you bring a paper bag into the kitchen. I smell fresh bakery stuff, maybe bagels. Probably onion."

"I'll be damned," he muttered.

"You probably will be if there's no lox," she added, mock-stern.

"What's a bagel without lox?" he quipped.

"So when do we eat?"

"Any time you're ready, darlin'."

They ate the bagels and lox he brought, then he spent part of Sunday reading to her the Sunday *Times* he'd picked up at his apartment. She helped him with the crossword puzzle.

During the course of the day Mark attempted to forget what he'd seen behind the closed door. He thought he'd succeeded. He made love to Judith later that afternoon and in evening as if she were a fragile piece of glass. And then, with desperation.

Judith fell asleep enfolded in Mark's arms.

SLICK. ICY. *No way to slow down. Out of control. Impact.* "No!"

At first she didn't know what had awakened her, or why. Perhaps it was the unfamiliar presence of the man sleeping at her side. She just knew that something was terribly wrong.

Can't . . . Please, oh, please . . . "No!"

She froze at the rasping groan, so raw and terrible that it sounded as if it had been torn bleeding from his throat. "Mark?"

She could feel his thrashing around, then heard another groan. She reached out, finding him, only to have him push her away. The rejection hurt until she realized that he wasn't aware, or awake. Above all, he needed help—and she was the only one able to give it. What if he were desperately ill and she couldn't do anything? For the first time in a long time she roundly cursed the darkness.

Pull yourself together, she ordered herself behind gritted teeth. The last thing he needs is a hysterical female. Judith moved as close to Mark as she dared, aware that the spasmodic flailing of his powerful arms could hurt her. She didn't care.

"What's wrong?" she asked. He was shaking and clammy with sweat. His chest heaving, his breath uneven, the sound coming from his throat was almost a sob. She couldn't stand it. He was stiff, tense, agitated, unresponsive, almost as if she weren't there. When he struck out at her again, she wasn't afraid. But she knew that she wouldn't be able to find out what was wrong with him, or help him, until she had stilled the violent thrashing of his body. And there was only one thing to use—herself.

She anchored his head by placing her palms on either side of his face. She laid her cheek against his, felt his movements slow, then still. "Wake up, Mark," she begged hoarsely. "Oh, please, wake up." To which she added the desperate inner plea, "Don't let him be sick."

He didn't know where he was, or who he was with. The only sure, constant thing was the terrible familiarity that was present in the darkness of his mind. Judith. She had been in his dreams so often . . . she seemed so real. He felt her hands on his face, her arm across his chest as he struggled to drag breath into his lungs.

She heard his breathing change, slow to a more regular rhythm; the erratic gasping ceased. She smoothed his hair and stroked the taut planes of his face. "What's wrong, love?"

She bit her lip in frustration as she felt him turn his head away. "You don't have to tell me, Mark. I won't press. But I do know that keeping things inside doesn't help. It festers, eats away at you." She heard him swallow. "Do you want to talk about it?"

"No."

She stiffened, feeling left out, unable to share in things.

He could feel her hurt, though she said nothing. And he realized that he would have to speak, even though for him, it was salt to an open wound. "It's just—a dream," he said finally.

Could a dream have done this to him? It wasn't just a dream. Then she remembered. "Not just a dream," she said, instinct driving her on, "this was one of the nightmares you told me about, wasn't it?"

"Yeah," he admitted resignedly.

She knew of only one thing that could have affected him so deeply. "About . . . the accident?" She felt him stir restlessly in her arms.

"Yes," he said brusquely, concentrating all of his efforts on trying to make the terrible images fade from his consciousness.

She heard him take a shallow breath. And she did nothing but stroke him, in an effort to comfort him.

She hadn't pressed, but suddenly the barrier that held the words back seemed to give way. "It's always the same," he said, taking a deep, resigned breath. "That damned hill.

I keep waiting for the ending to change. If I'd done anything different—"

"No."

"But it always ends the same way. I can't get you out of the car. I *can't*."

"But you *did*, Mark. You did."

"No."

There was only one way to silence him, to stop the words. She kissed him.

He felt the hard-wired tension inside himself relax as he returned her kiss, losing himself in her generous warmth.

He calmed.

"Can I get you anything?" she asked softly as she felt him relax beneath her touch. "Coffee? Warm milk? A drink?"

There was a heartbeat of silence. "You. Just you."

Her mouth found his again.

He savored the warm wetness of her, feeding, then quenching fires coursing through him. A seamless circle of unending, passionate love.

It was so good to be held.

7

THE WEEKS THAT FOLLOWED that first rapturous weekend together had been a time of discovery for both Mark and herself, Judith mused as she logged in a message for a Personal Touch client. Despite the fact that she and Mark had come together in the greatest intimacy a man and a woman can know, both agreed that they had a great deal to learn about each other, and even about themselves. And the learning process itself was magical. . . .

They both enjoyed theater, although she tended toward the contemporary stage, and he favored the classics. They determined a mutual affinity for music. Judith found Mark loved opera and symphony as much as she did; they passed many golden hours exploring each other's CD libraries—as well as each other. Judith's latent love for baseball surfaced, and when they attended Orioles games, Mark was her own personal play-by-play announcer.

They explored the gamut of regional and ethnic restaurants in the area. But often, a fun date involved her cooking dinner for him—or he, for her. Her specialties included pastas. And Mark often seemed to favor dishes that were hot enough to merit a five-alarm rating.

Sometimes it was almost as if the outside world didn't exist.

"Personal Touch, may I help you?" Judith answered, automatically turning to her braille typewriter so that she could document the umpteenth call of the frantically busy morning. She relaxed again when the caller turned out to be Maggie.

"I just wanted to know if Leo and I should call the police," Maggie said dryly.

"What!"

"We haven't seen you in so long that we thought Mark might be holding you for ransom."

Judith leaned back in her chair, laughing helplessly. "What would you pay?" she gasped when she finally managed to control some of the mirth that kept bubbling to the surface.

"How about having dinner tonight at Chez Sullivan?"

"Can I bring a friend?" Judith asked coyly.

"Does the friend like prime rib?"

"And Yorkshire pudding?" Judith prodded, her mouth already watering.

"Would I make one without the other?"

"Never." Then she asked, "What time?"

"Six okay with you?"

"I'll have to call Mark and get back to you."

"Well, we can forget about dinner, then."

"Never mind." Judith chuckled. "What can I bring, Maggie?"

"Besides Mark?"

"I was thinking of dessert," Judith quipped. And knew from the warmth of her cheeks that she was blushing, thinking of the many times that dessert had been a sensual, rather than an edible feast.... She cleared her throat. "I'll bring a cake."

"Your extraspecial, never-fail orange glaze cake?" Maggie asked eagerly.

"How can I disappoint such a gracious hostess?" Judith replied.

MARK WAS looking over the fine print of a soon-to-be submitted proposal when the phone rang. He glanced up, knowing that very few people had access to his private line; most calls went through Sarah. When he picked up the receiver and said hello, a smile automatically slid into place. And broadened as he heard Judith's voice in response. "How's everything at Personal Touch?" he asked.

"Busy-crazy. How's high-tech city?"

"Same. Hey, it's your nickel, darlin'."

How she loved the sound of that drawl! "About dinner tonight—"

"Is there a problem?" he asked, devoutly hoping she'd say no.

"Not exactly. Except that we've been ordered, uh, invited to dinner at the Sullivans'. They think we've been deliberately avoiding them."

"Now, how could they have come to that conclusion?" Mark asked, pretending innocence.

"Haven't the slightest idea." Judith laughed as she informed him of Maggie's offbeat invitation. "You can see why I think we have to show up."

Laughing, too, by this time, Mark allowed that he understood why she'd felt compelled to accept. "Yeah. It sounds like an offer you couldn't refuse. And I guess I have been keeping you pretty much to myself."

No more than I've been keeping you to *myself*, Judith added silently at the other end of the line. Without meaning to, she and Mark had been existing in a delicious vacuum, reveling in an explosion of sensuality. His voice broke into her thoughts as he asked what time he should pick her up.

"Dinner's at six. How about five-thirty?"

"I'll be there."

"You don't mind going?"

He gave a short laugh. "I didn't say that. I'll even bring the wine. But this isn't a fairy tale, and I can't barricade us both in my castle. Not that you're not a princess," he added.

"And you're definitely a nut!" she said, laughing, her mind already starting the countdown for Mark's arrival.

"Can we make it a short evening?" Mark asked hopefully.

Judith didn't mind; she found his reluctance to break their pattern of exclusivity wholly endearing. "We'll tell them you have an early bedtime."

"Wait till I get my hands on you," he growled, mock-stern. "You are no fairy princess, lady. You are a witch!"

THEY HAD NEVER been together, the five of them. Robbie was there, too. That's why the dinner hour was set so early, Judith knew. She wondered how Mark would react to being part of the group; she needn't have worried. He seemed perfectly at ease. In fact, the tone for the evening was set when Robbie asked Mark for burgers and fries!

"No way, son of mine," Maggie said immediately. "And no finger painting for dessert!"

Everybody roared except Robbie, who wanted to know why not!

Dinner was easygoing, conversation never lagged. And when the prime rib and trimmings had been thoroughly decimated, Maggie went into the kitchen to get after-dinner coffee while Judith went to work on the dessert.

"The cake's on the counter to the right of the sink," Maggie told Judith matter-of-factly. "And the knife's at three o'clock."

"Thanks," Judith said as she began to slice the cake.

"What's Mark's latest offering, Judith?" Maggie asked, as she went to pour brewed coffee into a heat-proof carafe.

Judith paused in the act of slicing, knowing that Maggie was referring to Mark's habit of bringing something almost every time he came to her house. "Yesterday it was a gardenia plant," she said, the memory of her delight uppermost in her mind. "And last week he gave me a set of wind chimes and hung them on my deck." Already Judith was accustomed to the silvery sound they made as they trembled in the wind. She could also feel their shape, run her fingers over the cool metal cylinders.

During the past few weeks Mark had become so much a part of Judith's life that sometimes it seemed to her he'd always been there. They had dinner together several times a week, breakfast on mornings after. And the best time was the too fleeting interval in between, when they scaled the heights in each other's arms.

Judith forced herself away from thoughts that were too personal to voice, even to as good a friend as Maggie. "He never comes empty-handed, Maggs. He's always got something." And it seemed as if whatever Mark brought, it was something designed to appeal to her sense of touch, taste, smell or hearing. Sometimes all four. "I swear, sometimes I feel like Robbie. I open the door for Mark, and instead of saying hello, I feel like saying, 'What did you bring me?'"

"Why don't you say it? He'd probably get a kick out of it."

"Maybe I will." Judith laughed. "He's not what I expected," she continued. "He's big and strong, and quiet—but so dear. Sometimes it scares me to care about him so much. I don't know how to handle it."

"Very carefully," Maggie said quietly.

"There's no smile on your face, is there, Maggs?"

"No, Judith. None at all." She drew a deep breath. "Well, let's get this stuff trayed up and into the dining room before the troops get restless and attack."

"Do I get coffee, too?" Robbie asked as his mother carried the oversize tray into the dining room.

"Sorry," she replied. "Milk. Chocolate, if you want. But you've got to wait a few years for coffee."

Mark was working on a large slice of Judith's cake, enjoying the banter that went around the table, until Robbie started talking about his class's field trip.

"Guess where we went, Aunt Jude?"

"Haven't a clue, sport," she replied in the act of lifting her coffee cup to her lips.

"We went to see the new sculpture garden at the museum."

There was a deadly silence—big enough to sink a battleship.

Hearing all the things that were unspoken, Mark turned to Judith in time to see her deliberately set her cup down in its saucer. "Damn," he muttered under his breath, feeling Judith's tension. He surreptitiously covered her hand with his own. "Judith—"

Her slender back was rigidly erect, stiffly elegant. He ached for her, hated not being able to say anything. But he couldn't, of course. It would only make Robbie feel bad, and it wasn't the child's fault. He was used to prattling on, telling all kinds of things to Aunt Jude.

Bolstered by Mark's support, Judith took a deep breath and forced a smile to suddenly dry lips. "Tell me about the sculpture garden," she encouraged.

"I'm sure Robbie would rather play a computer game," his mother cut in hurriedly.

"But I want to tell her, Mom. She likes art stuff. And besides, I don't want to play a computer game."

"I don't need to be protected anymore," Judith told Maggie in quietly definite tones. "Go on, Robbie. Tell me all about it."

"You wouldn't believe it, Aunt Jude. The sculptures, they were almost as big as the dinosaurs I saw out on the grass when Mom and Dad and I went to Washington. 'Cept the dinosaurs were neater, because you can ride on them."

"I bet they were," Judith agreed, carefully hiding the smile that threatened to break through at the thought of anyone riding a massive contemporary sculpture.

"ROBBIE DIDN'T mean anything," Leo said softly as he walked her to the door at the end of the evening.

Judith heaved a sigh. "I *know* that, Leo. And for Pete's sake, don't say anything to him. I don't want him to be all hesitant and fidgety around me."

"Okay, honey."

Judith shrugged. "It doesn't matter, really. It's not that big a deal. I would have found out about it anyway. I just overreacted. I'm sorry."

"*I'm* not the one affected, Jude," Leo said softly.

Judith came to attention. "What do you mean?"

"Maggie would tell me to mind my own business."

"The heck with that. It's Mark, isn't it? He tried to comfort me after what Robbie said, and I just turned him aside. Damn. He doesn't deserve that," she muttered, gnawing on her lower lip.

"You'll find a way to make it up to him."

"He does so many things for me," Judith said, her voice so soft that Leo could barely hear the words. "And I care about him so much."

"ARE YOU ALL RIGHT?" Mark asked Judith once they were back at her house.

"Sure."

Right, he jeered inwardly. She was stiff as a board, stretched tight as a drum. And he didn't know what to do for her—or if she would even let him try.

To his surprise, *she* tried to comfort *him*.

"Mark, what happened tonight didn't bother me. Really."

"Is that why you had to fight off tears, why you were shaking?"

"I was startled, and I overreacted, that's all. I'm fine now. And don't think for a moment that I brood about art all the time. I don't. I've accepted my limitations, I really have. It's just—sometimes, when I get caught un- awares—" She heaved a sigh, certain from Mark's lack of reaction that he didn't believe her. She would have to prove to him that Robbie's remarks didn't mean anything to her. Very determinedly, she made light of what the boy said. "Not to worry. Sculpture's not my thing, anyway. I'm much more interested in the work of art at hand right here."

He scanned her living room, wondering what she meant. "I like the way the place is decorated, Judith, but damned if I can see any work of art."

"Ah, but you don't see what *I* see," she murmured softly, stretching out her hand. Her fingers discovered his jaw, then tunneled farther back, firmly anchoring in his hair. "This is the kind of art I'm interested in." She increased her efforts, focusing only on Mark and the pleasure she could give him, determined to drive every other thought from his mind.

"I can't think when you do that," he groaned, turning his head until his lips found the pulse throbbing at her wrist.

She put her other arm around his neck, then leaned forward until the tip of her tongue was just grazing his ear. "Good."

EVERYTHING SHOULD have been wonderful. It should have been. It wasn't. He had seen Judith. Met her. Conquered her hatred. They had become intimate. He thought she had come to care for him. And he knew he was crazy in love with her, even though he was certain it was too soon to tell her that.

But no matter how wonderful the present was, no matter how close he and Judith became, Mark could never seem to let go of the past. He had stupidly thought meeting her would assuage his guilt. It hadn't. It had brought him closer to it. He could never quite forget his conjured vision of Judith Blake, the artist. He had only to remember the room—that damned room.

He was tortured by her inability to paint, at the lack of art in her life. And now, the harder he tried to forget, the clearer the image became emblazoned in his mind: the "ghost of Judith's past" that he had conjured in his mind, sitting on a stool, brush in hand, oblivious to anything but canvas, paint and design.

He would have given anything to be able to restore what she'd lost—what he had taken from her. He'd seen her works on display; that only made his inner pain worse. Judith not painting was like a great concert pianist suffering from arthritis and not being able to use his hands.

Robbie Sullivan's innocent remark was a catalyst, bringing to the surface of Mark's mind all that he had unconsciously tried to suppress—all that was tearing him apart. But in the days that followed, he wasn't able to shunt it aside. There was only one thing written on the blank slate of his mind. Deep inside of him was a primal urge, an urge to give Judith back her art. He wanted her to be back where she belonged, in the art world, enjoying the success she had worked so hard to attain. There was only one problem. She had accepted her disability; he had not.

Mark's engineering-trained thought processes automatically downshifted into problem-solving mode. Whether alone, with business associates or even when he was with Judith, one part of his mind was concentrating solely on the intricate riddle that seemed to have no solution—how to reunite the lady with her art.

Sometimes he despaired of ever finding a solution to the problem he'd set for himself. *You* want Judith to paint. Go ahead and tell her that, why don't you? The bile rose in his throat at his own monumental conceit. Here he was, concentrating on phantoms, callously ignoring Judith in the process. You're a fool, Leland, he derided, disgusted at his own effrontery, not a miracle worker.

The more muddled his thinking processes became, the more intense his frustration. But just when he was convinced he would never reach a solution, it all came together, jerking him out of a restless sleep.

He was sprawled in bed, Judith tucked securely against his side, but he came awake instantly, as if a light had exploded in his head. At first he was disoriented, knowing that nights like this usually led to his nightmares.

Easing away from her, he snapped the light on, wondering what had awakened him in the gray dawn of early morning. But there was no nightmare this time, only the glimmer of an idea that left him cold and shaking. Disbelieving his own temerity, he dragged a hand through his hair, then stared blankly at his fingers.

"All right," he muttered as ideas ran back and forth in his head as if he were seeing them projected onto a screen. Judith was blind. He forged ahead, ignoring the pain the word caused him. She would never see again. But there was nothing wrong with her hands.

She did all kinds of things with only the assistance of her hands that sighted people normally did with the assistance of vision. Pouring drinks, lighting candles, baking a cake. Only she used her sense of touch as a guide. That's it, Mark exulted to himself. Her hands. Or, more exactly, her fingers.

They were strong, slender, capable. He remembered the way she had helped the boy finger paint. She could feel the colors. No, he corrected himself—she could feel the paint. And he was sure that she could still handle a brush.

Ideas began to filter into his head—ideas on how a person could paint using touch instead of sight. He remembered his vow that he would do anything, give anything, if she could paint again.

Saying nothing to Judith or to anyone else, he bought a variety of materials at an art-supply house, then realized that he'd have to make a trip to the hardware store, too.

It was only after he'd given the paint-by-touch method a crude try himself that he felt ready to test the device on the person it was designed for. He picked up the phone, his fingers automatically punching out Judith's number.

SOMETHING WAS WRONG with Mark. Judith had sensed his preoccupation all during the past week and more. He had called her less often, broken two dates because of work—an engineering problem, he'd told her.

But it was never more evident than at dinner this evening. She had spent more time than usual in the kitchen. Coq au vin wasn't exactly the easiest thing for her to prepare. But from the way she could hear him picking at his food, she could just as easily have given him a cheese sandwich on day-old bread.

And then there were those silences, which stretched to monumental proportions. When she tried to make conversation, Mark was totally abstracted, as if he were off in another dimension. Or maybe he just wished that he were, Judith mused bleakly as she sat back, lost in thought beside her virtually invisible lover. Maybe he was trying to let her down easy. . . .

"I brought you something."

She snapped to attention, so lost in morose thoughts that she hadn't even been aware he was speaking. "Dessert?" she asked, deliberately infusing lightness into her voice.

Mark almost lost his carefully held composure. "Not exactly." He felt a tremor the length of his body. "I'll get it."

He went to his car to bring in the bag of paraphernalia that had cost him so many agonizing days, sleepless nights and time spent away from Judith. Before giving it to her, he felt like saying, "Close your eyes." He swallowed, handing her the bag.

She took what he handed her. From the feel of it, it was a wrinkled paper sack filled with oddly shaped objects. Puzzled, she opened the sack and rummaged inside. Her fingers had no trouble identifying what he had brought with him: a small jar, a paintbrush, a spool of wire and a box of nails. When her fingers closed on the largest object, she immediately identified its familiar shape and was stunned. She pulled out—of all things—a canvas that had been altered in some way.

For the life of her, she couldn't fathom why Mark had brought her a painting that she couldn't see. Charming idea. And then she felt the odd configuration of nails around the canvas's edge, and wires strung across its surface. "What is this?"

"I'm not sure what to call it, except—" He cleared his throat. "This is the problem I've been working on all this time."

"*This* is your engineering problem?" she asked, her voice rising in amazement.

"Oh, please," he groaned, looking above for divine assistance. Nothing happened; there was no miracle at hand. It was just like the night of the accident. He would have to do the rescuing, but he himself might not survive the conflagration. "It's . . . for you to use."

"To do what with? I don't understand."

Mark took a deep breath. "It's—it's a way for you to paint by touch."

Mark could sense her withdrawal even before he had finished speaking. His heart sank as he saw her face whiten and her body freeze into immobility.

At first Judith said nothing. She couldn't. She was shocked speechless. When she found her voice again, she didn't bother to mince words.

"Are you out of your mind? Is this some kind of sick joke?" she demanded, her voice trembling. "Are you testing a new sense of humor? If you are, don't test it on me. And I guarantee you won't win any prizes as a stand-up comic."

"I wasn't trying to be funny."

"How about cruel?" she cut in, hating the way Mark had made her confront herself, reminding her of her deficiencies. "How *dare* you make me remember that other world? I miss it all—the smell of paint, the feel of the brush in my hand, the turpentine, the media. And the colors...oh, my God! The memories won't go away. But I don't live in that world anymore. I *can't*. And wishing won't make it so," she snapped, "no matter how we might want it otherwise."

Mark had spent so much time and effort devising the method, he hadn't even stopped to consider that she would refuse it outright, rejecting it, and himself. He was deeply hurt. But he wasn't about to give up without a fight.

"Judith, let me just explain what I've done. You could think of painting in terms of shapes, rather than colors."

"I'm not interested."

"You're going to listen," he said evenly. And then, with great patience, he told her of the system of painting he had devised for her. "I took a canvas and hammered small nails, several inches apart, into all four sides of the frame. The nails anchor the wire. I've stretched wire to form a grid. When you paint, you use the edges of the grid as a guide for your hand."

Judith said nothing, simply shaking her head. "I think you're certifiable, Mark."

He ignored her last remark. "You're not the only one with a disability, Judith."

"Are you going to tell me that Beethoven was deaf?"

"I'm going to tell you about artists—Renoir, Degas, Matisse. They were all disabled toward the end of their lives. And none of them ever stopped creating."

"Amazing. All that creativity, and not one of them had Mark Leland to prod them into action." Then, in the heat of the moment, she dismissed his idea as foolish, unworkable, ridiculous. "You're chasing rainbows, Mark, tilting at windmills. I don't want to paint again."

"What about the finger painting sessions you have with Robbie?" he asked, clutching at straws.

"A parlor trick," she tossed back at him.

And then, sensing the undercurrent of hurt and pain in Mark's voice, Judith deliberately used a softer tone to tell him how she felt. "I'm—I was used to freedom, to working unrestricted, flowing paint as personal expression. Your method...your technique is too mechanical. It would strangle me. I'm not an engineer. This is *your* world. It's not the way I create. Just because alternative means worked for Degas, Renoir and Matisse doesn't mean they would work for me."

She knew she had hurt him. It cut both ways. She was hurt, too. There was no point in prolonging his pain, or her own. "Mark," she continued gently, "the world I once knew—the art world—it isn't mine anymore. It's closed to me. I can't live there. I can't be part of it. I've accepted that, and I've accepted my limitations. Why can't you?"

He couldn't. It hurt too much. She'd given up. He didn't consider that he was being totally unrealistic to expect her to stick her neck out, to step off a cliff into nowhere. "I'm sorry, Judith. I didn't mean to rake up the past. I thought maybe I was blazing a trail into the future. I—oh, hell. Just take the stuff and trash it."

"Mark, I know you meant well, and I do appreciate it."

Mark fought against a tide of crushing disappointment. "Sure." Then, because he no longer had anything to lose, he decided to go for broke. "You won't even give it a try, will you?" he asked quietly, his voice laced with sadness.

"I *can't*," she whispered brokenly.

"You know what, Judith? You're selfish. You've got all this creativity locked up inside of you, but you'll only let it out if it can be on *your* terms. You can't paint in the traditional way, so you've closed the door on anything to do with art. Somehow, I didn't think that you were that full of self-pity." Then, realizing he'd said a great deal too much, he left her house without saying anything further, not even goodbye.

She heard the soft click of the door, and then silence. It wasn't until after she heard his car engine start that she realized she had no idea if he was coming back....

8

MARK JUST DIDN'T understand, Judith told herself. She was a colorist. The subtle permutations of the spectrum were paramount in her work. Everything else, even the ultimate shape of the design on the finished canvas, was secondary.

If she were to paint using Mark's technique, she would have to go from being a colorist to working almost exclusively with shape, possibly geometric. Painting is the relationship of one shape to another, Judith thought to herself. She always knew the boundaries of the canvas, bisecting it with wide swathes of color. *Had* known, she corrected morosely.

She'd accepted her condition, accepted the fact it would never change. Did she have the courage to try to reopen a wound that had never really healed? It would be better not to make the attempt, rather than for her to try and fail. And how would she even be able to judge what she had accomplished? It was hopeless.

Judith found that she couldn't sleep. She could also blame that on Mark; she wasn't used to sleeping alone anymore. She ended up leaving the bedroom and making her way down the hall to the studio she hadn't used, or even entered, in more than a year.

She opened the door and froze. She'd never brailled the room, she realized as she stumbled over a can of paint. "Slow," she told herself, "just take it slow."

With measured steps, she walked the inner perimeter of the room, then made her way carefully through the mine field of the relics of her lost career. In her wanderings, she skimmed the surfaces of empty canvases, the dust on the palettes. She picked up a soft sable brush, stroking her face with it. And she recalled Mark's pain when she wouldn't listen to him that night they first had dinner together—and now again. He was just as human as she.

She went back downstairs to the living room, realizing that the objects Mark had brought were still there, silently mocking her. They were there, and Mark was gone. Already she missed him. She no longer felt whole without his presence, she acknowledged bleakly. Even when they didn't make love, she enjoyed just being near him, being held, and holding him. And worst of all, she had hurt him, which was like hurting herself.

So as a kind of apology to Mark, she took the jury-rigged collection of paraphernalia that was his "invention" and went back up to the studio. To her amazement, walking through the door of the room was easier the second time around.

She set Mark's gifts on her old sketching table, and then slid onto the well-worn stool that had been her favorite spot for so long. Taking a deep breath, she picked up the altered canvas. She quickly discovered that Mark's technique was crude, intended more for a precision engineer like himself than an artist. "Nails around the edges of the frame," she muttered under her breath. Wire and paint. What a combination! She would feel more like a technician than an artist.

And the canvas itself was unprimed. She turned it this way and that in her hands, her fingers tracing the pattern created by the crisscross of the wire grid. Working between the spaces of the grid was like trying to find a place on a map.

Her fingers sought the brush he'd provided. She smoothed its tip, quickly discerning that it was nylon. She recalled how the brush had once been an extension of her hand; together, hand and brush had seemed to direct themselves across the universe of the canvas. No more, she thought grimly, setting the brush down. She had taken her gift for granted, never dreaming that it wouldn't always be there. She remembered things she had wanted to do that would now never be done.

But Mark's technique *was* unusual, and showed a great deal of imagination. The colors would be flat, of course, she mused, because there could be no shading, no depth, no perspective. She couldn't handle those kinds of subtleties by touch alone.

Next, she twisted the cap off the jar of paint. The smell brought back the sharp sting of memories that had never quite been eroded. She dipped the brush into the jar. With her left hand, she lightly touched one of the vertical wires that went from the top of the canvas to the bottom of it. And with her right hand, she tried to lay color onto the gridded surface, using brush strokes that were as natural to her as breathing. Then she shifted her left hand to a different wire, and started the process again. "Awkward," she muttered as she felt paint glob all over the grid and her hand.

She had no idea what she was creating, or even what color paint was in the jar. She'd never even bothered to ask. But the very act of applying paint to canvas, even the simple act of holding the brush transported her back in time. When she'd finished, her heart was fluttering and her mouth was dry.

There were enough negatives, the biggest of which was, how could she possibly know what a painting looked like? There were probably more negatives that she hadn't even thought of. But then there were the positives—things that other people in her position wouldn't have access to. She had a memory of color, an instinct for design and arrangement. Maybe—just maybe—she would be able to change her style of painting to suit what she *could* do.

The bottom line was Mark's technique was crude and would certainly need refinement, but it worked! Judith's fingers tingled as she remembered what it felt like to hold a brush again, to create, even though she couldn't see the results. And when she had more paints, the whole spectrum of premixed colors to work with . . .

She closed her eyes tightly, pretending for a moment that when she opened them she would be able to see. She opened her eyes, seeing only blackness, as usual, but somehow it didn't seem as deep or as empty as it usually did. She felt a rush of exhilaration; it was almost like making love.

Her instinct was to pick up the phone, punch out Mark's number and shout "Eureka" in his ear.

Judith wiped damp, shaking palms against the sides of her slacks. She wasn't going to tell *anyone* about the grand experiment. Not yet. Not until she knew if the technique worked in practice, as well as theory. And maybe not even then . . .

Too tired to shower, Judith washed her face, brushed her teeth and put on a nightshirt. She set her clock for seven-thirty. With any luck, she could be at the art-supply warehouse by nine. And then she crawled into bed, willing herself to forget how much she missed Mark's form next to her.

"GOOD MORNING, Mark. Here are your messages," Sarah said as her boss walked in somewhat later than usual. "Do you want me to hold your calls or cancel any meetings?"

"Why?" he asked as he flipped through the stack of pink notes she'd handed him.

"Because you look like the morning after the night before."

"Or like I've been on an all-night bender."

"Have you?" she asked drily, a frown of disapproval clearly on her face.

"No, Sarah. Alcohol is not responsible for my appearance."

"Ah." She nodded wisely.

"Or that, either!" he snapped, knowing that she was probably picturing a genteel orgy. "Maybe it would have done me some good," he said with a shrug.

"Which?" she asked, tongue in cheek.

"Never mind," he growled. When she turned away from him, he heaved a sigh, shaking his head at the way he'd snapped at her. "Hey, Sarah—don't go away mad. I'm sorry."

She retraced her steps. "What's the matter?" she asked softly.

"I'm just trying to work out a problem," he said, mentally referring to the mess he'd made of his relationship with Judith. He'd hardly slept the night before. And he couldn't very well tell Sarah that he'd had the nerve to order Judith to use the Rube Goldberg creation he'd devised. Well, hell, he couldn't even use it himself, and he was sighted!

"Do you need a sounding board?" Sarah was asking.

"I need a lot more than that," he said with a humorless laugh. "I'm an engineer. Problem solving is my business, but some things just don't have solutions."

"Some things just need time, Mark. Try putting it on the back burner for awhile," Sarah suggested as she turned to make her way out of the room, closing the door behind her.

It would probably be on the back burner forever, he thought, looking longingly at the phone.

He called her at ten after nine. There was no answer.

JUDITH WAS at the entrance of Farrington Art Supply by nine in the morning.

Suppressed excitement quivered in her as she greeted familiar staffers whom she hadn't spoken to since before the accident. They were surprised, but happy to see her. She'd been one of their best customers. They were only too glad to fill her order for everything she needed. They even helped her with braille labels for the jars of acrylic paints she selected.

From there, she took a cab to the hardware store, buying a hammer, a pound of small nails and several different kinds of wire. Then she was ready for the grand experiment. But she knew it might only raise false hopes that would hurt worse than treks to different doctors in fruitless attempts to restore her sight.

By the time she got back to her house, it was long past lunchtime, but for the first time in more than a year and a half, Judith felt the raw edge of excitement. Ruthlessly ignoring her need for food, she pulled the stool up to the drawing table and started to work. She would succeed, she told herself—not only for her own sake, but because she knew what it would mean to Mark.

"WORK?" JUDITH SNORTED nearly three days later. What she was doing was carpentry. Bad carpentry. How could she use Mark's technique if she couldn't manage to get the nails into the edges of the canvas without totally smashing her fingers, or destroying the canvas itself in the process?

Her frustration knew no bounds. Mark's invention didn't work. Paint spattered across the damned grid when she finally did get one canvas wired up; she could feel excess blobs all over it. She tried starting again, but the results were at least as bad. She didn't know what the paintings looked like, but she was sure they were awful.

Then, in desperation, she tried painting free-form, not using a grid at all, but couldn't control the brushwork, lost track of the design and even had trouble remembering what colors she had chosen. And worst of all she couldn't let her imagination roam free as she used to.

As tears of frustration welled in her eyes, she felt like throwing the canvas across the room and sweeping everything from the oversize table where she worked. She'd discovered early on that painting over the gridded surface was a two-handed process, which necessitated a flat surface. She couldn't even use a damned easel, like a normal artist.

But you're *not* a normal artist, an inner voice taunted. You're just doing some fancy form of occupational therapy.

She came within a hair's breadth of trashing everything, as Mark had suggested. Her pride wouldn't allow it. Despite what he might be thinking of her now, she was no quitter. But pride wasn't going to help her paint again, Judith admitted reluctantly. Whether she liked it or not, she needed help. Nibbling on the end of a nylon sable brush as she used to do, she considered, and rejected, one possibility after another.

She could ask Leo, but she wasn't about to tell him or Maggie about the "grand experiment." Her mind nearly rejected one other potential candidate: Mark. She wasn't ready to tell him she was trying his technique, let alone needing his help to get started. But she really didn't have a choice. With a heavy sigh, she put down her paintbrush and picked up the phone....

MARK WAS AFRAID that his clumsy foray into the art world had permanently alienated Judith from him. Since he'd given her the painting method, their relationship had been strained, at best. Only two days ago he'd spoken to her on the phone, asking her to dinner. He'd wanted to apologize for causing the scene in her house, and more than that, for trying to impose his will on her. The tone of their conversation had been excruciatingly polite, as if they'd never met face-to-face, let alone known exquisite intimacy.

"Could we make it later in the week, perhaps?" Judith had asked hesitantly, her mind's eye picturing the newly purchased paraphernalia that littered her studio. "I'm kind of snowed under. I need a few days to sort things out."

"Take all the time you like, Judith."

"I'll give you a call when my desk is clear."

"I won't hold my breath," he'd muttered after hanging up the phone.

He hadn't called her since. So when the phone rang and Sarah told him that Judith was on the line, he was tempted to say, "Take a message." Hell, since he'd met Judith, his pride had been battered into insensibility, and the gauge on his common sense supply read empty. If he had any pride or common sense, he would for once listen to his brain, not his heart. He'd suffered enough rejection at her hands to last a lifetime. But pride or no, he was simply not strong enough to resist the shaky words he heard her struggle to say over the phone: "Mark...I need your help...."

JUDITH SNAPPED to attention at the sound of the doorbell. Sighing resignedly, she set aside the canvas she was trying to work on and went downstairs to let Mark in. He hadn't asked why she needed his help, but had answered in a flat, unemotional tone, "I'll be there in about an hour."

There was a greeting on Mark's lips. It died as he stared at Judith's face—at the streak of blue on her cheek, and the multicolor smudges on her oversize shirt and tight-fitting jeans.

She heard him start to speak, then wondered why he'd stopped in midsentence. "What's the matter?"

"What the hell is wrong with your face?"

"Wh—what do you mean?" she stammered.

"Maybe it's a new shade of blusher or something."

"Mark, will you please try talking in English?"

"You've got blue paint on your face," he whispered hoarsely, feeling more than a little dazed.

"Oh, I didn't know," she said weakly, her hand automatically searching for the spot he mentioned. One of his large hands captured hers. She felt his other hand gently stroke her right cheek. Her throat tightened as she realized his hands were shaking.

"And a rainbow of colors all over your clothes," he added, almost afraid to believe what he was seeing. "Judith, why didn't you tell me?" he inquired, hurt that she hadn't seen fit to at least let him know she'd been trying the method he'd devised. And then, as he watched her standing poised as if for flight, his spirits plummeted to new depths.

"It didn't work, did it?" he asked in a low voice, his hands falling away from her. "I put you through all this for nothing, made things worse for you. No wonder you didn't want to hear from me again." He drew a deep breath. "I'm so . . . I'm so sorry—"

"No!" she cried, her hand instinctively going to his mouth to muffle his words. "I . . . it *does* work. I mean, I think it will if you can help me get the hang of it, maybe modify it a little."

The fleeting touch of her fingers on his mouth was almost enough to drive everything else from his mind. Almost. "If it works, if you can really paint, why didn't you tell me, put me out of my misery?"

"Because I couldn't get it to work, no matter what. I was going to call you when I finally finished a painting, but I couldn't even get started—not really, I mean. I'm about as handy with a hammer as an elephant with a toothpick." She felt his tension, reached out to caress his tightly clenched jaw. "I needed help, and was too stubborn to ask for it," she admitted, bowing her head.

Unable to resist, he turned his lips into the heart of her paint-stained hand. Now it was a working hand. He closed his eyes, breathing a silent prayer of thanks. "Stubborn lady. Is that all?"

"And because what I'm doing isn't art," she mumbled. "Not yet, anyway."

He responded with a crude four-letter word. "You don't mind if I have a look for myself, do you, darlin'?" he asked rhetorically, capturing her hand as he determinedly pushed past her into the house. He took the stairs two at a time, Judith trailing in his wake. When he reached the threshold of the room that had caused him such pain, he froze. Then he forced himself to walk inside, where he gazed spellbound at the pile of paint-smeared canvases stacked haphazardly in a corner, and at the blank canvas lying on her worktable.

"It's just an experiment," she cautioned.

"And I've been beating my brains out," he muttered as he hauled her into his arms.

"Don't come near me." Her words were muffled against his chest.

He felt a stab of pain, until she went on to say, "I'll get you dirty."

"The hell with that!" he growled as he dragged her into a crushing embrace that lasted until neither had any breath to spare.

"Judith," he gasped finally.

"Hmm?" She clung to him, so emotionally wrung out that she wasn't sure she'd be able to stand on her own if he took his support away.

Very gently he led her to the stool, his hands spanning her slender waist as he lifted her up and onto the seat. "Sit, darlin'. I just want to have a look at what you've done."

"They're awful. None of them are even finished."

Ignoring her words, he went to the corner of the room and hunkered down to look through the stacked paintings he'd noticed earlier. Even his untrained eye could see that her efforts were raw, almost primitive. Hell, so what if they weren't finished. He didn't care. He was ecstatic that she'd tried his method, no matter what results she'd achieved. The lady had guts. He swallowed, but despite his best efforts, his throat tightened and his eyes began to burn.

From her perch, the only sounds Judith heard in the room were footsteps and erratic breathing. Mark said nothing. Judith couldn't have found her own voice if her life depended on it. But the longer the silence lasted, the more nervous she became. "Well, say something," she rasped finally, climbing off the stool to find him.

He had come full circle, was standing near the entrance of the studio. "Mark, *please*," she begged, "I know they're not what I used to do, but are they that bad?"

His throat working, he had to struggle to force the words past the lump in his throat. "Wonderful. It's—" And then, because he couldn't control his emotions any longer, he tried to turn away from her.

Her heart constricting, Judith's arms automatically encircled him, urging him closer. She pressed his face into the hollow of her throat, moaning softly as her skin was dampened by the warm wetness on his face. "Oh, my dear—"

"Sorry," he gasped, striving for control.

"Are you all right?" she asked, one hand gently stroking his hair, intent only on comforting him.

"Getting there," he managed, his hoarse voice reflecting the emotions he felt at the joy of discovering she'd tried his method. "I'm getting there. You don't know what this means to me. When you called, I never dreamed—" He drew a deep, shaky breath. "Wow." For a long moment he just stood there, savoring the wonder of having her in his arms again. And then he remembered her phone call. "You said you needed help."

"Expert help. I discovered I'm less than swift at hammering nails. And aside from that, the wire's awfully stiff, and I've ruined a lot of canvases, and I want to make it work."

"All right. I get the picture." He smiled at the groan Judith uttered at his pun. "But you're the expert, darlin'. You tell me what you want to do, and we'll see what we can come up with. Tell me what the problems are and then what you'd envisioned," Mark encouraged, hoping he would be able to translate her ideas into a technique she could handle.

"Well, I don't think the wire works real well. It's too hard, inflexible. It makes the paint glop and run together when the brush hits it. As for what I envisioned, I guess at this point I was hoping to do something with colors in geometric shapes and patterns. Then, when I finally start something on canvas, I can't keep track of the design. And that's about all I can tell you," she concluded with a sigh.

"I'm going to have another look at what you've done."

"Oh, Mark, they're awful," she moaned.

"Hey, I'm a lowbrow. I won't know."

Getting her approval, he began by studying one of her canvases, noting how the colors had mixed. He knew she didn't want that. He saw how the paint seemed to wobble. Maybe wire wasn't a good idea, he mused, racking his brain for substitutes. "How about string? Soft twine. It would be quicker for you than using wire, and more flexible. You can wind it around just by feel."

"Hey, that sounds great! Why didn't I think of that?"

"'Cause you're not an engineer, darlin'." Pawing through her supplies, he tried to come up with other ways she could achieve control of paint, brush and canvas. There were brushes of all sizes, jars of paints, a heavy-duty stapler, masking tape, tools whose uses he couldn't even begin to understand. . . .

Thoughts flashed in and out of his head.

"Mark?"

"Huh?"

"I didn't hear anything. I thought maybe you'd fallen asleep."

"I couldn't if I wanted to. I think an idea is beginning to flicker in my mind."

"What kind of an idea?" she asked excitedly.

"Shh. Not yet. Hang on a second."

She heard his rummaging, then the sound of the stapler. "What are you doing? You sound like some kind of a crazy woodchuck or something."

"Or something," he muttered as he started using the stapler. "Y'know, I think I'm getting the hang of this. Do you reckon da Vinci started this way?"

"Lunatic!" she said, laughing. "Keep working."

"Slave driver." By this time his jacket and tie were long gone, his shirtsleeves rolled up past powerful forearms.

"Gripe, gripe, gripe."

"Okay. Back to your worktable, lady. Tell me what you think of this." Without saying anything further, he grasped Judith by the shoulders and propelled her to the stool in front of her worktable. "Sit."

She sat, tenderly amused at his enthusiasm.

"Here."

He'd handed her two canvases, one with nails, and no wires, and the other with staples and tape. "Okay, I give up."

"Aw, gee, I thought it was obvious."

"Mark, if you don't tell me what this is, I'm going to bite you."

"Promise?" he teased. "Okay, let me put you out of your misery. I can see why the wires were more trouble than they were worth."

"Hey, don't say that. They got me started."

"Yeah, well, the wires weren't an end, honey. They were just a beginning, a jumping-off point. This way, all you have to do is paint between the rows of string, which is more flexible than wire. And on this other canvas you can use masking tape to mark off areas. The staples that run around the edges are a kind of braille ruler that you can use to align the tape evenly. I'll fix up as many canvases as you want. And that's it, I guess."

She wasn't saying anything, just running her fingers over the two canvases, pausing every once in awhile. And the longer she kept silent, the more nervous Mark became. "Judith, for pity's sake, would you please say something?"

"Turnabout's fair play," she said smugly.

"Judith!" he roared.

"All right, all right. I can't believe it!" she exclaimed excitedly. "I think I actually understand what you're getting at. I can paint stripes, or geometrics, and then mask the painted area and start all over again. And if I thicken the paint, I'll be able to feel the edges of the color I'm laying down. Oh, wow!" she breathed.

"I think you've got it, lady." Marveling at the look of wonder on her face, he took a deep breath. "When are you going to try it out?"

"What's wrong with now?" she replied, her fingers automatically locating a jar of paint and a brush.

Fascinated, Mark watched as she painted a strip of deep red color next to the masking tape on the canvas under her hand.

"How do you know how wide the color will be?" he asked, never having seen an artist work before.

"The width of the brush governs that," she said absently. She tested the painted area with a finger. "Rats. Not thick enough. Boy, is this going to be a slow process."

"Why?"

"Because I have to wait about thirty minutes for the first strip to dry before I can tackle the next one. But hey, am I complaining? No way! Mark . . . where are you?"

Taking a step forward, he had to clear his throat before he could answer. "Right behind you. Looking over your shoulder." He hoped she didn't mind. He didn't think he could ever get enough of watching her paint. For him, it was like the culmination of a dream. . . .

OVER THE NEXT FEW WEEKS, Judith's concept of the mechanics of her art underwent a radical transformation as she discovered that painting by touch alone was by no means easy. Instead of focusing on colors and shadings as she used to, she was forced to think in terms of shapes and textures. And she could no longer paint with abandon, her imagination running free, her hand operating almost independently. By trial and error Mark helped her devise a means of remembering the designs she conceived, and the colors and shapes she used to execute them.

But in spite of all the help he gave her, and all the moral support, her first results were—at least in her own mind—unsatisfying. Judith painted slowly but steadily, deriving some measure of inner satisfaction from the fact that she was working again, but privately wondering if anything would ever come of it. At times she feared she would hate all of her efforts. But in her more realistic moments she reminded herself that even in the best of times, Judith Blake had always been her own worst critic.

Little by little the number of discarded canvases became fewer, and groupings of partially finished works began to occupy familiar spaces on easels around the room. It was like blazing a trail, she realized. No, she corrected, it was like breaking trail, taking a first step in a snowdrift. The first step was always the hardest.

She had felt herself sinking under the weight of self-doubt. But practice had made it easier. She was learning to tell the quality of her work by touch. And then one day Judith felt that peculiar rush of exhilaration that told her that the canvas under her hand was right. Real. Good.

For the first time since the accident, she was whole again. Useful. She was doing what she was meant to do—paint, even if she couldn't use the delicate shadings of color that had once been her trademark.

When Mark came to Judith's house that evening, he was tired from a long day's work and problems that wouldn't quit. He figured he and Judith would maybe have dinner and he'd read snippets of the evening paper to her. And later...

Judith was waiting for him at the door. "I almost called you this afternoon."

Her face was turned up to his. It was probably a trick of the light, but he was sure there were stars in her eyes. Bending his head, he touched his mouth to hers. "Call me any time."

"This wasn't something for the phone."

"What's wrong?" he asked quickly, his heartbeat accelerating. There was something odd about Judith, but he couldn't figure out what it was.

She took his hand. "Come upstairs with me."

He thought she was leading him to her bedroom. She halted in the carpeted hallway, at the entrance of the studio.

"There's a painting on the easel near the door. A *finished* painting. I—" She swallowed hard. "Just take a look at it."

"It's—" His eyes blurred momentarily as he focused on the first work of art she'd completed in more than a year. "It's wonderful," he exulted, whirling her into a dizzying dance of joy that left them both breathless. "Hell, it's a miracle!" he panted.

"I've got a long way to go, Mark. This is just a start."

"Some great philosopher is supposed to have said that every journey starts with a single step. Well, lady you've just taken a giant step back into the art world."

"Oh, Mark..."

"Trust me," he breathed, yielding to gravity as he slowly sank down to the carpeted hallway, Judith still clasped in his arms.

"I do. And I want to thank you for every—"

He kissed her into silence, ravishing her mouth as his hands tenderly caressed every part of her body. "I need you," he groaned, the words raggedly torn from the depths of his being.

"No more than I need you," she murmured, her fingers seeking and unerringly finding the hem of the sweatshirt he wore, and dragging it over his head. When she fumbled with his belt buckle, he set her hands aside, dealing with his jeans and briefs in one motion, then with the paint-spattered clothes she wore.

"I can't wait," he ground out, his control almost nil.

With consummate skill, she found his groin, her heartbeat speeding up to match the heated throbbing she held in her hands. "I need you, too. Please, oh, come to me," she implored, her body arching helplessly toward him.

"Easy, love. Easy," he crooned, aching with need as he laid her carefully on the carpet, then held himself tautly over her.

His hand went to her center, her legs parting to welcome him. With a gentle finger, he found she was throbbing and moist. "Soon," he hissed, swooping to ravish her mouth as his other hand tenderly cupped the thrusting firmness of a breast. She jerked helplessly at the sensual tension, crying out at the inner fires he had kindled.

He held back as long as he could for her sake, but her legs locked around his back, her tongue plunged deeply into his mouth and her palms kneaded the muscularity of his chest; her nails lightly grazed his nipples, giving no quarter. Her name a tortured groan on his lips, he surged deep into her velvet darkness with a passion made all the more fervent by the compulsion to celebrate her new work of art.

His head fell forward, coming to rest on the pillow of her breast. He tried to move, knowing he was too heavy for her, but the passionate cataclysm had exhausted him beyond movement. "Did I hurt you?" he asked when he had finally recovered and was able to speak.

"I don't know," she answered, her mind still reeling at the memories of the exquisite spikes of pleasure that he had sent coursing through her. "Am I black and blue?"

"You're beautiful," he said, tenderly pushing the damp hair from her forehead. "But," he said, helping her to her feet, "you're going to be sore and carpet-burned if we spend much more time on this rug."

"I think there's space available in the room down the hall."

They made love in her room, in the dark, so that they could be equal. They fell asleep in each other's arms.

Never leave me, his mind entreated before sleep overtook him, obliterating everything but her presence beside him.

Don't ever let me go, she mouthed against his chest as the darkness of sleep transcended the darkness of the constant night.

Mark's excitement about the paintings was eclipsed only by his desire for the painter. He had succeeded beyond his wildest dreams—he'd brought art back to Judith Blake, and made love to Judith Blake, the artist. Throughout the night he explored her softness, devoting himself to her until she caught fire in his arms and he went up in flames in her.

Judith felt desire, want and need come together in an expansion beyond anything she had ever experienced. She had never known that feelings, too, could have colors....

9

"YOU KNOW WHAT you've got to do now, don't you?" Mark asked Judith after they had showered together the next morning.

"What?"

"You've got to tell Leo and Maggie."

"About what?" she asked, deliberately choosing not to understand what he meant.

"Three guesses, Judith."

"Why?" she questioned him bluntly.

"You have to ask? They care about you. They worry. You're their favorite topic of conversation. The longer you wait, the harder it's going to get," he coaxed.

"What if Maggie doesn't like what I've done?"

"Has she ever *not* liked what you've done?" he countered.

"She's been known to criticize," Judith said diffidently.

"Sounds like another person I know. You. Call her, darlin'," he urged.

"When I get some more paintings done. Maybe that one was just a fluke."

"No way!"

"All right, it wasn't a fluke. I'll call them soon."

MARK HELD OFF after that, waiting, watching as the number of canvases gradually increased. When Judith had finished eight more paintings, he once more suggested that she call Leo and Maggie. "Waiting won't make it any easier, y'know," he prodded gently.

With a smothered sigh, she reached for the phone.

That same evening Leo and Maggie came to Judith's house expecting good food and good conversation. They weren't prepared for the course she served up after dessert.

Judith took Mark's hand for comfort. He squeezed her fingers in encouragement. "Go on, love."

Judith took a deep breath. "Would you both come upstairs with me. I—" She swallowed hard. "There's something I want to show both of you."

Maggie looked at Leo, who shrugged. Then both turned and followed Judith and Mark up the stairs, and stared when they saw Judith and Mark go into the studio.

"You . . . want us to come in there with you?" Leo asked softly.

"Yes, please," Judith said.

He motioned Maggie to enter before him, then wondered why she stood frozen in the doorway. He edged past her, and saw paintings he'd never seen before. "What the—" He spun on his heel and saw Judith, white-faced, Mark's arm around her shoulders. "Are they yours, Judith?" he asked, his voice shaky.

She licked her lips, which were suddenly dry. "Yes."

"You painted them?" Disbelief, curiosity and a burgeoning feeling of wonder warred within him.

"Yes."

"Before the accident?" he prodded.

"*No.*" The denial came from Maggie, whose gaze hadn't wavered from the paintings in front of her.

Judith winced at the sharp edge she heard in Maggie's voice.

"How do you know?" Leo asked, turning to his wife, who was staring wide-eyed at the display of paintings neither had ever seen before.

"Because I know her style better than just about anyone, except Judith herself." The new works were much smaller than the mammoth twelve-by-eighteen-foot canvases that had been her trademark. The colors Judith had used were jewellike, their effect almost sensual to Maggie's experienced eye.

Maggie tore her gaze from the paintings that mesmerized her to focus her attention on Judith. "How long has this been going on?" she asked with deceptive softness.

Judith winced at the unspoken hurt in Maggie's voice. "Several weeks."

"And you didn't feel you could tell Leo or me?"

"It wasn't that—"

"Where did you get this idea?" Maggie continued, as if Judith hadn't spoken.

Judith leaned her head on the shoulder of the man beside her. "From Mark."

"She's not exactly the confiding type, Maggie," Mark was swift to point out. "Tell Leo and Maggie what your reaction was when I explained the method."

"Umm . . ."

"She's so shy and retiring," Mark said with a wry grin. "In a nutshell, she told me I was certifiable. I assumed she'd trashed the whole Rube Goldberg idea, until she called me and yelled for help with it."

"I'm sorry, Maggie," Judith began.

"We'll see if you really mean that. How many paintings are there?"

"What you see is all I've done so far. Just nine."

"Just!" Maggie muttered under her breath. "We'll need more," she continued matter-of-factly.

"For what?" Judith wanted to know.

"I'm your agent. Yours is not to reason why. All you have to do is paint. A lot. When can you have more canvases ready?"

"Why?"

"Just like Robbie," she grumbled, mock-stern. "Always asking why. So I'll give you the answer I give him: *because*." And then, seeing the frown on Judith's face, she added, "I've got some bare spots on my walls—these paintings are the perfect size to fill in the gaps."

"You're kidding," Judith sputtered.

"Oh, you don't like that explanation? Well, try this one on for size. I'm going to earn some commissions."

"How?" Judith demanded.

"By selling some paintings."

"Oh, Maggs, they're not good enough. You're just saying that to get even with me for not telling you I was working again. You're not really serious about this."

"I'm not? Leo, tell Judith if I'm joking."

Leo was leaning against the wall, struggling with shaky emotions, while at the same time enjoying every minute of Judith's after-dinner treat. "She looks dead serious to me, cuz. As a matter of fact, I try not to get near her when she has that certain look in her eye."

"Oh, no, " Judith groaned. "I know that look. It usually translates into 'I told you what to do. Now do it.' Did anyone ever tell you that you were bossy, Maggs?"

"Yes. You, Leo, my son, and I'm sure Mark will get around to it when he knows me better. Now stop trying to change the subject. I'm still your agent. I get a healthy percentage of everything. It's time we started saving for Robbie's college education. He's going to be going to a *very* expensive school," she said, flashing an impish smile at Leo and Mark. "Now you know why I need these paintings from you."

And then Mark had to release Judith as Leo and Maggie came over to envelop her in hugs.

JUDITH AND MARK had eaten out, then gone back to his high-rise condominium, which was near Johns Hopkins University. She had been to his place so often that it was almost as familiar to her as her own home.

When the phone rang, Mark grumbled, before stretching out an arm to pick up the receiver. "What?" he demanded curtly, glad that the phone hadn't awakened Judith, who was tucked snugly against his side.

"Wake her up," he heard Maggie say.

"Maggie," he whispered, "can't whatever it is wait until morning?"

"Look, I know your love life is important, but if you don't wake Judith, I can guarantee she's going to have you for breakfast."

Resisting the temptation to tell Maggie how intrigued he was with the thought, he gently kissed Judith into wakefulness.

"Mmm."

"Phone, darlin'."

"What?"

He hoisted the sleepily protesting Judith into his naked lap, tucking the receiver against her ear. "It's Maggie."

"What?" Judith mumbled, smothering a yawn.

"I'm going to need about forty-one more paintings."

"For your walls?"

"Not my walls," Maggie replied cryptically.

"Okay, I give up. You've got a secret, right?"

"I've got good news, Madame l'Artiste. You're committed to a one-woman show at the Centre Gallery."

Judith was too shocked and dazed to say or do anything. The phone dropped from her suddenly nerveless fingers.

"What's wrong? What happened?" Mark asked, concerned at her sudden pallor and the way she sagged against him. He braced her against him as he replaced the phone in her hand.

"A show," she gasped, breathless with disbelief. "Maggie's booked me into a one-woman show at the Centre Gallery. I can't believe it. It's only about two weeks since she first saw my paintings."

"Terrific, darlin'," Mark exclaimed softly, giving Judith a loving squeeze.

"Are you there?" Maggie asked.

Judith cleared her throat. "I'm here," she said her voice emerging hoarse and strained anyway. "A show? Really?"

"You haven't had a show in a while," Maggie was saying. "It's about time, I think. And Henry Carter thinks so, too."

So Maggie had been talking to the director of the Centre Gallery.

"The show will be on November twenty-first. That leaves you almost four months to do the rest of the paintings. I'm sorry for the short notice—someone else cancelled."

Everything else that Maggie said after that about publicity, interviews, the date of the opening, all sailed over Judith's head. She was a working artist again!

"You've got a good start, Judith. Now keep going. if you need some help—"

"I can do it myself, Maggie."

"She'll have all the help she needs," Mark spoke into the receiver, assuring not only Maggie, but the woman he held in his arms.

The next morning Judith turned to Mark as they walked into the studio. "Do you think the show will be a success?"

"You bet."

"But—"

"Hey, don't borrow trouble. Do what Maggie says. Get to work."

Judith picked up a fresh canvas, then set it down again. "What did you mean when you said I'd have all the help I needed?"

"I work cheap," Mark quipped.

"You?"

"Don't sound so shocked—I'm insulted."

"I didn't mean that I don't want your help, but you're working."

"So are you," he pointed out.

"But—"

"Hey, I've helped you before. If necessary, I'll take some time off from work."

"You will?"

"What have you done about Personal Touch?"

"I'm taking a leave of absence, you know that."

"Is there any reason why I can't do the same?"

"But you head your own company."

"At least I don't have to ask the boss for permission to take some time off. Let me make a couple of phone calls to get things set up at the office, and then you can show me how you want the canvases prepared."

AFTER THAT, things snowballed, with Judith and Mark working in tandem. He continued modifying canvases for her and even kept her stock of paint supplies replenished. And she worked harder than she ever had in her life, planning the designs and executing them.

Her concentration paid off, because with the euphoria that came with the return of her ability to paint and create, Judith was able to immerse herself in her work as she had always done before. In short order she created *Intermittent Blues*, which was a study in pure color. In *Crystal Dreams* she tried a kaleidoscope of different hues. And *Phantasy* was a study in layers of paint, which created their own flow of shapes.

She no longer needed the morning light that had been so important to her when she had been sighted. She could work around the clock, if she wished. Screening out everything but brush, canvas and palette, she ignored the time of day, the need to eat, the people around her. Only there had never been a Mark Leland in her life before. More often than not, he turned up in the studio when she was working. When she had painted before, she recalled, interruptions had been the bane of her existence. With Mark, she didn't seem to mind, somehow. Why was that, she wondered.

Whenever possible, Mark was there, helping Judith in any way he could, getting a tremendous amount of satisfaction out of contributing to her work process. In addition to preparing canvases, he moved them out of harm's way when work on them was finished, and took them to the gallery. And he helped her with braille labeling of paints and media.

And sometimes he just stood in the doorway, arms crossed over his chest, watching her work. It was a miracle to him—the slow, precise way she laid out her design, worked out the colors, applied the paint and finished up each canvas.

But his hardest job was the self-appointed task of taking care of Judith herself. She had to work slowly and carefully, concentrating at all times. The result was a growing stack of well-executed paintings, and an artist who was often tired and tense to the point of exhaustion.

Mark did everything he could to make Judith's life easier as she worked toward her deadline. He made sure that she ate, carried her to bed, massaged the stiffness from her taut muscles and held her when she was too tired to do anything but collapse. He watched her lose herself in her work, and knew that he had done what he'd set out to do: give her back her art—at least in some measure.

But in spite of everything, he couldn't make her reduce the harsh inner pressures she imposed on herself. And on more than one night, he extended a hand and found the bed empty next to him. He never had to wonder where she was. He knew.

"She's pushing too damned much," he finally growled. He couldn't remember when she'd had a decent night's sleep. And the time to stop was now, he decided as he went in search of her. He didn't have to look far, just across the hall from the bedroom.

"Trying for the *Guinness Book of World Records*? Seeing how late you can stay up?" he asked.

"I had an idea that wouldn't quit. You know what I discovered, Mark?"

That you love me, he said to himself. "What, darlin'?"

"When I painted—before—I'd lay in the dark, just on the edge of sleep, or wake up in the middle of the night, an idea for a painting full-blown in my head. Well, the same thing's happening now. And Mark, I used to have to wait till morning to try an idea out. Now I can do it anytime!" she exulted.

He caught his breath as her words cut him like a two-edged blade, at once depressed and elated. She had left him for a canvas and paintbrush. He had given her the means to do that. It was because of him that she could paint around the clock. And it was because of him that she didn't have to wait for the morning light. "But why are you pressing so hard? You're falling off the perch." Which was his way of saying that she was decidedly wobbly on her stool.

"To make up for lost time. I can't work as fast as I used to."

"Honey, you've nearly finished all the paintings you need for the show. At the rate you're working, you'll have enough for one, maybe two more shows. You're tired, darlin', out on your feet. Give it a rest."

"I'll never finish on time."

He smothered a sigh, knowing how tense and brittle she was. "Yes, you will. You've got over a month." She was also losing weight, and there were shadows under her eyes. He was afraid she would collapse under the pressure she was putting on herself.

"Just let me finish this one." Then, muttering a curse, she flung aside the painting she was working on.

"What's wrong?"

"I screwed up the damned painting. It was going so well. It would have finished up this series, and I just screwed it up."

"What's the real problem, honey?" Mark asked gently.

With a deep sigh, Judith set down her brush. "I'm frustrated because I can't keep track of my designs well enough. I can't judge my work by anything but memory of the original plan. I guess it's sort of like losing work in your computer. Well, it's just something I have to get used to. Not to worry."

"I guess it would be better if you could make sketches, huh?"

"Well, I can't," she said gruffly, turning her attention back to another canvas she'd been working on.

"How do you usually keep track of the paintings when you're working on them, and then after that, when they're finished?" Mark persisted as he set staples in two-inch increments around the edge of a canvas.

"By making braille notes and a braille label for each canvas."

"But how do you know what each painting looks like once you're finished with it and the paint's dried?" he persisted.

"I remember," she said stiffly, busying herself with laying out a pattern of vertical stripes on the fresh canvas beneath her fingertips.

"Right, I understand that, Judith. But, honey, you've finished maybe forty paintings. What's going to happen when you get to a hundred and nine?"

"I'll think of something." She shrugged, trying not to grumble at his well-meant interruptions. "Now, do you mind if we have a little quiet, before I mess up for a change?"

The next day Mark found his mind working overtime again. By evening he had tentatively worked up a method for Judith to keep track of her painting designs by using coffee stirrers and rubber bands glued to small pieces of poster board.

The stirrers represented straight-edged divisions between bands of colors on her canvases, he told her, and the rubber bands were curves. And the color in each area could be noted on braille labels and applied to the sections of the canvas. "They're not to scale, exactly, but I can work on that."

"Who cares about scale?" she cried as she locked her arms around him, hugging him as tightly as she could. "You're a genius!"

He let his mouth descend to hers. "I was inspired."

BUT EVEN MARK'S "inspiration" didn't keep Judith's anxiety at bay for long. He didn't know what he was going to do about it, but he knew he was going to do something.

"You need a break, Judith."

"I don't have time for a break."

"At least come away from the studio, just for a while."

When she finally agreed, he took her out for breakfast the next morning—and afterward kept right on going.

"Isn't it taking a little long for us to get back home?" Judith asked.

"Just sit back and relax, darlin'."

"I don't feel like relaxing, Mark. I feel like painting. At my studio. At my house. *Now*."

"Sorry. No can do."

"Why not?"

"Because we're not going home."

"Why?"

"Because you need a break, and you won't get one in your studio."

She was furious. "Are you crazy? I have work to do. You have no right to do this," she hissed.

"I know. But have you gotten much done lately? You've had to trash your last three canvases."

"That's a low blow."

"You're too tired to hold the brush."

"I want to go back home."

"Nope."

"I'll call Leo and Maggie the first chance I get."

"Feel free to call them, darlin'. By the way, Maggie packed your clothes for you. I hope she didn't forget anything."

"You had an accomplice, huh? Well, I'm not going to like this one bit."

"Okay, have it your way. Hate it."

"Where are we going?"

"Oh, you're finally asking?"

"Where, Mark?"

"Wait and see. Now, why don't you lean back and try to get some rest."

"I'll quit while I'm behind," she muttered, scrunching all the way to the right of the car seat, until she was virtually fused with the door.

Judith roused herself when the car came to a final stop and got out without waiting for Mark. A soft breeze pulled at her hair, whipping it past her cheeks. The air around her held a salty essence she could both taste and smell. And her ears automatically contrasted the squawking of birds with the crashing of surf.

Entranced, she turned as familiar footsteps came around to her side of the car.

For a moment Mark panicked, overwhelmed by the audacity of the stunt he'd pulled in getting Judith to come with him. But then he decided that there was no point in holding back. "We're in Cape May, New Jersey. I wanted to bring you somewhere different. It's quiet here, and kind of elegant." The explosion he'd been expecting wasn't forthcoming.

"You've been here before?" she asked.

"Once, a long time ago, but in July, not September."

With another lady, Judith assumed.

"With my mother, before she moved to Arizona to live with my aunt. Mom wanted to come back to the place where she'd honeymooned with my dad. Would you rather go somewhere else? I mean, there's always Atlantic City, or Ocean City, but I thought they were kind of noisy."

Poor thing. He sounded so hesitant, she thought, as if he were expecting her to get back in the car and barricade the doors. "No."

"No?"

"No, I don't want to go anywhere else. In fact," she lied blithely, not knowing quite why she was doing it, "I've always wanted to come here, but I never seemed to have the time. Show me Cape May, Mark," she asked softly, her hand outstretched. Immediately, her hand was engulfed in his as he drew her into a crushing embrace.

"You'll have a great time, Judith, I swear it. Still mad at me?" he asked softly.

"I—you know I don't like to be taken over."

"Hey, lady, I care about you. A lot. And it hurts me to see you working yourself into the ground."

"But—"

"And I'll tell you something else. I give you carte blanche to do the same for me if I become such a workaholic."

"Kidnap you and spirit you away to some secret destination?"

"Yeah," he growled, slipping an arm lightly around her waist. "Sounds like a great idea. Feel free."

"All right." She sighed, leaning back against the hardness of his chest. "Let's see where my captivity's going to take place."

Judith gave herself up to the enjoyment of the first real vacation she'd had in years. Mark plied her with food, took her dancing, made love to her halfway through the night. The world receded as she fell asleep in Mark's arms, the lapping of the waves a gentle counterpoint to the steady beat of his heart. It was close to heaven.

"Are you sorry you came?" he asked her as they walked barefoot on the beach the next morning.

"No. It's just . . ."

He dropped down to the moist sand, gently tugging at Judith's hand until she was sitting cross-legged beside him.

"What are you so afraid of that you can't even take off a day?"

"That I'll forget the method."

He kissed her fingers. "These fingers won't forget. You can practice on me."

She slipped her hands away from his, a smile tugging at her lips. "I think I'll practice on nature's canvas, thank you."

"I don't see—"

"Feel, Mark. Touch."

He looked down and saw that she'd created a rectangular frame in the sand in front of her, and was proceeding to draw.

He stilled her hands when she started to obliterate what she'd done. "Hey, don't erase the pictures."

"Oh, Mark, they're just mud pies," she dismissed with a shrug.

"They're pretty. They remind me of your finger painting. And don't tell me it's a parlor trick. Couldn't you do this with paint?" he asked, liking her fanciful works.

She shook her head.

"Why not?"

"I don't do sand paintings, that's why not."

"You're doing it now, though."

"Just to keep my hand in."

He groaned at her pun, then picked up her sandy fingers and kissed the back of her hand. "Judith . . ."

"I can't use finger paints on canvas, Mark. And if I used paper, the paint would be flat, and I wouldn't be able to feel the edges. Unless . . ."

"What?"

She shook her head.

"Why not?"

"I guess I could do a background in acrylic thickened with gesso, then work in the design. It would give the painting a textural quality, I think."

"It sounds like Greek to me, but if that's what it takes..."

"It wouldn't be hard. I could even add contrasting colors. Of course, it's not what I usually do. What if Maggie doesn't like it?"

"She's an agent, not an artist, darlin'," Mark said, wrapping his arms around Judith's slimness. "Go for it."

She did—back at the studio. Judith returned from Cape May rejuvenated, her hands tingling with ideas. Her fingers had *not* forgotten how to paint. Pushing herself to the limit, she screened out everything, concentrating on nothing but translating her memories into the movement of paint on canvas. The first thing she worked on was called "Seascapes." The companion grouping was "Sand Paintings." When she finished, she framed Mark's face with her paint-encrusted hands.

As JUDITH WORKED feverishly to put the finishing touches on the last paintings for the show, Mark inwardly conceded his relief that the pressure on her was coming to an end. He didn't have to probe too deeply into the recesses of his feelings to admit how much he missed the time they'd spent together.

"Face it, Leland. You're jealous of a paintbrush. You want her to have more time for you," he said to himself. No, it was more than that. He wanted them to have more time for each other, for things to be normal, to revert to their former closeness. And he started making plans—plans that would take Judith away from her studio and put her back into his arms. He stilled the ungenerous thoughts that filtered in.

Logically, he knew he shouldn't resent the fact that painting was once more the focal point of Judith's life. But emotionally he struggled, not content to be with Judith only when she had time for him. He tried to weave himself into the fabric of her existence, but often found himself gritting his teeth when she broke dates or painted through the night, or fell asleep when she was too tired to make love.

There would be time for togetherness when the paintings for the show were finished....

10

MARK FELT LIKE shouting hallelujah when he left for work one Thursday morning in mid-October, Judith's final paintings in the car and ready for Maggie.

Maggie wanted to know how Judith was.

"She's high as a kite."

"She'll calm down, Mark, don't worry."

He looked forward to taking Judith out to celebrate the completion of the paintings for the exhibit, but when he got to her house that night, she was so absorbed in the canvas on her worktable that she didn't even hear him come into the studio. He came up behind her, pressing a kiss to the back of her neck. "Hi."

"Mark!" she squeaked, nearly toppling off the stool. Only his steadying hands on her waist saved her. "I didn't hear you come in."

"I figured. I thought you were through. Working on something new?" he asked, deliberately keeping his voice light.

"Uh-huh." She turned her attention back to the canvas. "After you left this morning, I lay there in bed, and I swear I could see this progression of ideas in my head. I tell you, I was inspired. I wolfed down a muffin and parked myself on the stool. I laid it all out on a small scale, and by then I was so excited, I just had to start painting. I feel wonderful!"

She looked wonderful, too, an expression of rapture on her lovely face. She was positively blooming, even dressed in painter's garb, her hair all bundled into a shaggy top-knot.

"How about some dinner?"

"Not hungry. Maybe later. I don't want to lose my momentum. You don't mind, do you?"

He compressed his mouth into a straight line, then took a deep breath before answering, "No, of course not," and smothered his disappointment. "Can I fix you something?"

"No, thanks."

It was just a one-time thing, he told himself as he fixed himself a ham sandwich, washing it down with a cold beer. She was just caught up in the excitement of creation. He watched *L.A. Law* on television and tried to forget that the woman he was aching to hold was more interested in holding a paintbrush!

During that week Mark invited her to the sculpture garden. For Friday evening he proposed dinner and a tour of the Engineers Club. And on Saturday he suggested going to a wine-tasting at a Maryland vineyard. Her answer was always the same: she didn't have time. Dinners were forgotten. Postponed. She was too busy. She was always too busy, not to mention too tired to do more than sink into oblivion when she needed to get horizontal for a few hours.

He told himself he understood. The work was important to her. And to him, too, of course. But *she* was most important to him. Where did he rank with her? Did he have any importance at all in her scheme of things?

Mark, virtually on the ragged edges of her life, was annoyed at himself for feeling jealous. This was the way she *had* been—independent, gloriously fulfilled, in a way that had nothing to do with him. The passion and fire were all directed toward her self-expression.

He tried to ignore the incidents, kept adjusting, trying to accommodate his schedule to hers, attempting to coax her out of hibernation, certain that eventually something would work. He was at the office one day when he hit upon the perfect inducement.

His efforts had him on the phone the better part of the morning. When he told Sarah what he was trying to do, she only shook her head, the words "Mission impossible" on her lips. But when he left the office at the end of the day, he was able to tell her, "Mission accomplished."

"You're kidding!"

"Nope."

"Are you going to kidnap her again?" she asked wryly.

"No, Sarah. I doubt if I'd get away with it twice. But it *is* going to be a surprise. I'm just going to ask her to go up to New York City with me, just overnight. It won't take her away from the studio too long. She'll love it."

He didn't hear Sarah mutter, "Good luck."

That evening he asked Judith, "What would it take to pry you out of hibernation?"

"I don't know. What are you offering?" she asked slyly.

"My escort to the Big Apple this coming Wednesday. It'll help you recharge your batteries now that the opening is only three weeks away."

"Are you saying my batteries are dead?" she asked haughtily.

"Maybe a little weak, now and then. What do you say?"

"Umm . . ."

"We're only talking about overnight, Judith, not a cross-country trip. On the Metroliner. Dinner at the Russian Tea Room. A room at the Pierre. Chestnuts from street vendors . . ."

"It's too early for chestnuts."

"Okay, lady. Hot pretzels. I'll buy you hot pretzels."

"Stop!" she said, giggling. "You've hit me where it hurts. I'll go, I'll go."

His spirits leapt at the smile on her face, the rich sound of her laughter. It'd been worth it to have the phone almost permanently grafted to his ear that morning. "What decided you?" he queried, having deliberately omitted the pièce de résistance. That surprise was reserved for dinner conversation.

"The pretzels. I never could resist the smell of pretzels."

"Had I but known," he groaned.

"Thank you for asking me, Mark. And for caring," she said softly, sliding her arms around his waist.

"Comes with the territory," he murmured as his fingers gently removed the pins that kept her hair secured. "And how I love to explore it," he murmured as the dark, silky mass came tumbling down."

"But this time, I'm packing my own clothes."

"Yes, love," he replied obediently, his arms tightening around her. "Take something to dance in, hmm? It's been too long." Then he ventured to ask, "Are you at a stopping point in the studio right now?"

"Temporarily," she answered, her voice muffled against his chest. "I'm having 'painter's block.'"

"Come with me," he urged. "What you need is a good night's sleep."

She thought of the new series of paintings whose design had been eluding her for more than a week. Maybe Mark was right. Maybe she did need her batteries recharged. "Yes. It *has* been too long."

Neither Judith nor Mark had much sleep that night, or the night after. . . .

WHEN JUDITH AWOKE in the early predawn of Wednesday morning, she was pressed to the warmth of Mark's body, spoon fashion. Her body was nestled into the strength of him, his arm curved heavily against her hip, his palm resting on her belly.

Her instinct was to stay where she was. "No, be honest," she chided herself. She wanted to get even closer to him, to coax him into wakefulness, into making love with her. She knew from experience it wouldn't take much persuading on her part.

But equally strong was the feeling that somehow today was going to be different, special, if she could just keep that feeling of energy and well-being until she got into the studio. This morning—now, this minute—there was an edgy excitement coursing through her. Adrenaline was flowing. New ideas bombarded her from all directions.

Brushing a weightless kiss on her lover's shoulder, she edged carefully away from him. Then she pulled an oversize T-shirt over her head, smothered a yawn and headed for the studio. She picked up a brush, not for the first time enraptured by the wonder of being able to regain control of her work, primarily due to the use of the thickened paint. She was so excited she could barely hold the brush steady.

When Mark woke up, Judith's side of the bed was empty; that didn't surprise him. Nor was he shocked when he went into the studio and found her elbow deep in design sketches. "I thought you were having . . . painter's block."

"Not any more!" she announced gleefully, one paint-spattered hand gesturing around her. "I got up this morning, came in here, and all of a sudden, there it was—the solution to the problem that's been bugging me for days."

"Just think what kind of work you'll be able to do when you've really recharged your batteries."

She swallowed hard, knowing that he wasn't going to like what she had to say. "I can't go, Mark."

He stared at her in disbelief. "Why?"

"Because I've got work to do. I've just started on a new series of interrelated chromatics, and I have to do the paintings in a certain order for the master design to work."

"How long will it take?" he asked with a calmness he didn't feel.

"I don't know," she answered in a small voice. "You know how long it took me to come up with this idea."

Maybe it wouldn't have taken so long if she'd given herself a chance to live like a normal human being, instead of locking herself up in her studio almost twenty-four hours a day. But aloud, he only said, "What about New York?"

"It'll still be there when I finish this. Look, it's not as if the hotel reservations can't be changed. We could go some other time, when I finish these."

By then, he knew, another idea would be clicking into place, and another, and another. "I got theater tickets, too," he said resignedly, still not telling her the whole truth, certainly not what they had cost him in time and money.

"Maybe Leo and Maggie could use them. Why don't you ask them?"

Because they'd want to know why he was giving away two almost impossible-to-get tickets to *Phantom of the Opera,* one of the hottest tickets on Broadway. It was a show that he knew she was crazy about. She'd almost played a hole in the compact disc. He deliberately held back the name of the show, even now. He didn't want to bribe her into spending time with him. Hell, he didn't even know if a bribe would be enough! "I'll take care of the tickets," he said flatly.

"Mark, I'm really sorry. But I've got so much time to make up for."

He flinched, knowing that *he* was the reason that she had to make up the time. "I understand that, Judith, really I do. But why are you pushing so hard now, when your quota of paintings for the exhibit is filled?"

"Because all of a sudden the ideas are pouring in, and I don't want to lose them."

"But—"

"And besides, I need nine more paintings for the exhibit."

"Nine? But you've given Maggie the fifty she wanted. Did she renege on some of them?"

"No, but I want to do nine more to replace the first ones. When I started using the technique, the brush felt awkward in my fingers. Now I can replace those early, raw paintings with something better. Strike while the iron is hot." She sounded almost desperate.

A great weariness overcame him as he realized that he was doing more harm than good by arguing with her. "If you say so, Judith. You're the artist," Mark replied, his voice without inflection as he turned on his heel to leave the room. "If you need me, call me. I'll be working on a project at the office."

She turned back to her canvases.

He didn't come back.

MARK ATTEMPTED to shake off his despondent mood as he walked into his office. "Sarah, you need a couple of days off."

Sarah stared up at Mark, immediately noting the drawn look on his face. One thing was certain, though. *She* wasn't the one who needed the time off. "Really?"

"Call your husband and tell him you're going away together this morning."

Sarah got up from her chair and placed her cool hand on Mark's forehead. "Are you all right?"

He gently removed her hand, a wry smile on his face. "Fine. My treat. Consider this your Christmas bonus. And your birthday present," he told her, extracting an AMTRAK envelope from his pocket and tossing it on her desk.

"My birthday's not until February," she said automatically, her gaze not leaving him.

"Yeah, well, so I'm not big on calendars. Here are two tickets for the Metroliner. The train leaves at ten. There's a reservation for two at the Pierre. The theater tickets are on hold at the box office. Enjoy."

She picked up the AMTRAK envelope, recalling how excited he'd been about getting the theater tickets, how he'd been looking so forward to going with Judith. Sarah knew that he'd gotten box seats just so he could fill Judith in on the action of the play without disturbing other theatergoers. Sarah knew better than to ask Mark what had gone wrong with his plans. "I'll give you a check to cover everything."

"You will not. You will call your husband, go home and get dressed, and enjoy yourself and each other, and have a wonderful time."

Sarah shook her head as she watched Mark walk back into his office and shut the door.

The new beginning he'd envisioned at Cape May had been no more than a cruel illusion, a sea mirage. It was really an end. Once, he had thought that Judith had been the one woman with whom he could share his life. Now there was no room in her life for him.

If his rival had been another man, Mark might have stood a chance of being the victor in the battle for Judith's heart. But in trying to fight her all-consuming devotion to her art, he knew he was doomed to frustration. After all, he'd invented the technique that had given her wings. Now he couldn't keep her in a cage of his own making. He couldn't force her away from the studio. He would have to let her fly. He had no right to do otherwise.

In the days that followed, he initiated new projects at work, committed himself to a site visit, and generally focused on distracting himself with productive activities. His fatigue level increased. He was so tired some nights that he barely had time to shower before virtually collapsing on the too wide bed in his condo.

The anger and resentment over the New York trip had long dissipated. His seldom-aroused temper had cooled. He did anything he could to lessen the pain he felt as he forced himself to let his relationship with Judith taper off. But the pain didn't lessen—it seemed to deepen with every passing day.

THE UPCOMING SHOW was making Judith a nervous wreck. She'd been so enraptured with actually being able to paint, that she'd nearly forgotten about everything else, even the hanging of the exhibit itself.

"Today's the day," Maggie said when she called Judith the Saturday before the opening. "We're one week away. The paintings are going to be hung starting in about an hour. Do you want to be there?"

"Umm, no. But before you start, I have several more paintings."

"We're only hanging fifty."

"Right. I know. It's a long story. I'll ask Mark to bring them over."

"Judith, I want to know about those paintings!"

"Bye, Maggs," Judith said with a smile. Even though he'd been preoccupied with business commitments the last couple of weeks, Mark had been to her house twice. Once, to bring over art supplies from Farrington's and label them for her, and another time, to modify canvases with staples and nails. But he hadn't stayed long either time, both times pleading the press of work.

Mark had said she should call him if she needed him. As soon as Maggie said goodbye, Judith phoned his office and asked him about taking her through the gallery that night. There was the barest hesitation before he said he had a dinner meeting that would run late.

"Oh, no problem," she replied quickly. "How about tomorrow?"

"I'm sorry, Judith. I have to be in San Francisco for a site visit. I'll see you when I get back."

And up to that moment, he hadn't even mentioned that he had a trip in the offing. She had to clamp her tongue behind her teeth to stop herself from asking if he would be back in time for next Saturday's opening. "Have a safe flight," she said softly.

"Thanks."

Until now, Judith had been totally absorbed in her painting, oblivious to virtually everyone and everything around her. She had been so caught up in her work that she hadn't realized what was happening until it was too late: her relationship with Mark was deteriorating.

I'm losing him, Judith thought, her hand trembling as she hung up the phone. And I don't know why, or what to do about it. Was it lack of interest on his part? she asked herself. If so, then why had he pursued her the way he had, starting with the dance at the Engineers Club all that time ago?

Guilt was a distinct possibility, she told herself matter-of-factly. Physical attraction? Maybe. And since he seemed to be trying to get out of his relationship with her, maybe the real answer was that he had found someone else, the way her ex-fiancé Greg Hollins had. Greg was someone she had known in another lifetime, though. She had trouble remembering why she'd cared for him at all. She was not so lucky with Mark.

Judith slid off her stool, her hand massaging a nagging ache in the small of her back. Funny, that's the kind of thing Mark usually did for her, she thought absently.

What to do about the paintings, she wondered. She couldn't very well wait until he came back, not if she wanted them in the exhibition. The logical thing was to call Maggie.

"WHAT PAINTINGS were you talking about on the phone, Judith?" Maggie demanded as she walked into Judith's house.

"Hello to you, too," Judith said dryly.

"The paintings, cousin-in-law."

"I've redone some of the first paintings, the first nine, actually."

For the life of her, Maggie couldn't understand why. "But I already have all those pictures, Judith. Mark delivered the last of them more than two weeks ago. Are you working on a new project already? Why didn't you take a break?"

"Because the original paintings were raw, not as polished as the later ones. My technique got better—"

"They were not raw!" Maggie exclaimed. "Judith, Beethoven didn't trash his first symphony just because he wrote eight other ones. And why did you think I'd even let you replace them? The show's terrific the way it is."

"It's really important to me, Maggs. I've been working on them for the past two weeks, and they're done now."

"I'll look at them, and then decide, okay?" So many questions Maggie had to restrain herself from asking. Judith looked stressed enough. The last thing she needed was to be cross-examined. Stifling her abundant curiosity, Maggie invited Judith to dinner for Friday night, the night before the opening. "Feel free to bring your 'significant other.'"

"I—he's out of town, according to his secretary. I don't know when he'll be back."

Maggie stared at Judith, noticing how tired and drained she looked. At first she had attributed the tiredness to the strain of the upcoming interviews and nervousness over the opening itself. Now she wondered how much was due to Judith's working around the clock on this new group of paintings, and how much was due to whatever her friend *wasn't* saying about Mark Leland.

Why wasn't Judith talking about him, as she usually did? And why hadn't he brought over these paintings, as he had the others? Trying for diplomacy, Maggie stifled her curiosity, asking no questions at all.

"We should be through hanging the pictures by this afternoon, so we can do a walk-through tomorrow, Judith. I want you to know the arrangement of the pictures, the poster at the entrance, the banner hanging over the main entryway, even the publicity postcard with *Phantasy* on it."

"Do I get a guide?" Judith asked lightly.

"Me," Maggie quipped ungrammatically.

"Maggie, about the paintings, just make sure—"

"They're right side up," Maggie said, laughing.

"You read me so well," Judith admitted, laughing along with her.

"Practice makes perfect. I want you to get the lay of the land and to renew your acquaintance with the environs of the gallery." Maggie knew Judith hadn't visited it since the night of the accident. "It'll be better for you during the opening itself and, of course, during the interviews. Which will be on Monday, by the way."

The next day, Sunday, was crisp and cold. Maggie spent the better part of it helping Judith braille the exhibit space, the rest of the gallery and even the sculpture garden outside. She also briefed Judith on the two critics who would be doing interviews the following day.

"Groan." Judith was nervous about having her work exposed and laying herself open to criticism.

"WHAT'S THE MATTER?" Maggie asked Judith while they waited for the first interviewer to show up.

"Nothing. I'm just terrified about the whole publicity process."

"You'll be fine."

"They're going to think I'm some kind of oddity because of the way I paint. They'll be dissecting everything I say and do. I'll feel like a frog in Biology 101."

"It's no different than your other interviews."

"Oh, Maggie, come on. In my first show, I was one painter out of four. And in the second show—"

"You were at the top of your form," Maggie concluded for her. "And there's no reason to think you're not just as good now," she added in definitive tones.

"But it's still not the same. Oh, Maggie, tell me all of this hoopla isn't necessary," a weary Judith begged.

"Only as necessary as breathing," Maggie retorted. "If you want me to sell the paintings for you, they have to be presented right. We're not having a distressed-merchandise sale, y'know. Your paintings have to be showcased. And that means critics, champagne, hors d'oeuvres, working the crowd...."

"Ugh."

During the course of the interviews, Judith discussed each individual painting, and then explained the thematic connections between the groupings that were part of different series. She was asked to compare her earlier style to the way she painted now. To her surprise, she found she could be very matter-of-fact about it.

"In my earlier style, color was the focal point of each painting. Now, the union of color, shape and design is the cornerstone of my technique. And since I can't use perspective, I use thickness of paint to give the works a textural quality. The paintings themselves are tactile, as well."

"Do you always use the brush?" one critic asked.

"No. Sometimes I use a palette knife. And in at least one series of paintings, I used my fingers and hands."

"You finger painted?" the man asked.

"Yes," Judith replied, carefully concealing a smile at the obvious horror reflected in the man's question. "The two series called 'Seascapes' and 'Sand Paintings' were done using that technique, the media being acrylic and gesso."

"Don't you find finger painting...awkward?"

"No, but it is messy," she conceded.

One interviewer commented that it was fortunate that Judith had arrived at a new method of painting.

"I didn't do it on my own. The method was devised for me—" her mind struggled to fill in the blanks "—by a brilliant problem solver. He knew I needed help."

Somehow, it all began and ended with Mark, Judith mused to herself as the interview was finished, and she was finally able to go back to the studio and begin work on a new painting.

In recent weeks, Mark had been putting in a lot of hours on company projects, he'd told her. Oftentimes, when she asked him to dinner, he was too busy. And when they did have an occasional meal together, he seemed abstracted, somehow. And he didn't stay afterward. He called less and less often. And when they spoke, the conversations were often brief and unsatisfactory. And now he was traveling cross-country.

Maybe something was wrong with his business, and he didn't want to tell her. But whatever the reason, she knew that things between herself and Mark were somehow out of kilter, and she didn't know how to get them back on track. She only knew that the careful pattern she'd established for living—which for months had included Mark— was now out of sync.

What had life been like before him? Judith could hardly remember. It seemed so far in her past that it was a lifetime ago—someone else's life. It had seemed as if he were part of every phase of her being. He had even been responsible for her painting again. Maybe that had been his final way of salving his conscience.

Sometimes, in their now rare conversations or times together, she'd almost asked what had gone wrong. But her pride had squelched the impulse. She hadn't fought for Greg, she told herself. She wasn't about to start with Mark. Of course, she didn't bother to admit to herself that Greg hadn't been worth it. And Mark . . . With Greg, her feelings were hurt; with Mark, it was her heart.

All she had left was her pride and her prowess in the studio. Painting had always been her creative release, her outlet, the way her inner emotions were expressed. She reached for brush, paint and canvas, her hands shakier than when she'd first picked up the brush, weeks before.

After numerous false starts and increasing frustration, a frightening metamorphosis took place. The brush became a stick with bristles on one end. The paint was simply a jar of goo. And the canvas was like a black hole.

When she was calm enough, she tried again. The canvas remained as blank as her mind. Panic skimmed the surface of her mind as she tried different things, different approaches. She even played background music. Nothing helped.

The ideas weren't coming. She was like a dry well. It didn't make any difference *what* she tried. There was no joy in what she was doing. And what was the common denominator? she asked herself bleakly. Mark Leland. A tear rolled down her cheek as she put down the tools of her trade and left the studio.

"I understood Greg's defection. But why Mark?" she asked herself bleakly. "Why did he have to make me care?"

For what seemed like forever, Judith had kept panic at bay by remembering that Mark was a certain anchor in her dark world. More than anything, she wanted to know if he would be there at her side as she faced the opening reception with its hordes of people.

She hadn't heard from him since he'd left Baltimore the week before. She'd had the gallery send him an invitation, but she had no idea if he'd seen it. Gritting her teeth, Judith knew that there was only one way to find out. "Spineless weakling," she muttered. "C'mon, spineless, pick up the phone."

Judith hadn't been so nervous since she'd first gone to his office, months before. "Hello, Sarah. Is . . . Mark in?"

"I'm sorry, Judith. He's still out of town. He's in the San Francisco Bay Area. He's been in and out a lot, but I can leave him a message, if you want."

Three thousand miles away, Judith thought bleakly. "No, no message. Umm—do you know if he received the invitation to the opening?"

"It came before he left, and I handed it to him."

"Thank you, Sarah," Judith said dully.

Sarah had seen the suffering Mark had been going through and had been prepared to feel resentment toward Judith. But from the sound of the voice on the other end of the line, the suffering wasn't all on Mark's side. "Good luck at the opening."

Had that been pity in the other woman's voice, Judith wondered. Well, no matter. Judith didn't need sight to read the handwriting on the wall. If Mark couldn't even be bothered to come to her opening—to view the public's first glimpse of her work—then what did it all mean?

THE LAST PLACE Judith wanted to be that Friday night before the opening was the Sullivan house. She wasn't hungry, hadn't eaten much for days. And she didn't feel like being sociable, especially since the invitation had been for her *and* Mark. Even though Maggie knew that Mark was out of town, Judith was sure there would be questions about his absence so close to the opening. And she didn't feel like trying to come up with the answers. But for the life of her, she couldn't figure out how to refuse their invitation.

"Aunt Jude's here, Mom!" Maggie heard Robbie call from the living room. Wiping her hands on a towel, she went to open the front door. She was just in time to see a cab pulling away from the curb. Judith hadn't come by cab in a long time, not since she'd started seeing Mark on a regular basis. And Mark was nowhere in evidence. Maybe he was still out of town.

"I don't think I'm going to be very good company this evening," Judith apologized as she followed Maggie into the kitchen.

"You're not company, you're family," Leo replied, giving Judith a big hug. A feeling of worry gripped him as he noticed how much thinner she seemed to be. And her face was pale. For a person who would be achieving a major artistic goal in less than twenty-four hours, she was looking singularly depressed.

Over Judith's shoulder, he exchanged glances with·
Maggie. *What's wrong?* he asked silently. Maggie's answer was a helpless shrug. *Later,* she mouthed at him.

"Okay, you two. Break it up," Maggie ordered. "Leo,
would you please pour the iced tea? Judith can dish out the
salad. Everything's in the usual spot. Robbie, are your
hands clean?"

"In her other life, she was a general," Leo was heard to
mutter.

"Gripe, gripe, gripe," Maggie trilled, willing to play the
clown if it meant easing Judith's obvious tension.

With only slightly shaky hands, Judith served the salad.
It was going to be all right, she told herself. There weren't
going to be any awkward questions. She *would* be able to
get through this evening without any major disasters.

"Where's Mark?" Robbie asked between forkfuls of
shepherd's pie.

All·three adults stiffened. Leo and Maggie exchanged
helpless glances. Judith stopped picking at her food and
slumped back into her chair, hoping for a miracle that she
knew wasn't about to happen.

"He's out of town," Judith said, hoping for nonchalance, relieved that at least her voice was fairly steady.

"Is he coming back in time for the show tomorrow?"

Even though she was certain of the answer, Judith
couldn't bring herself to say the word. "Umm . . ."

"Robbie, let's change the subject. It's Daddy's turn to
talk. And I think he has a really funny story to tell us about
Jaguars. Don't you, *Daddy*?"

Gee thanks, light of my life, Leo groaned inwardly. "Judith, you'll never believe it," he said, jumping in with both
feet. "We've had some really good sales this summer."

"Grown-up talk," Robbie muttered. "Bore-ing."

Grateful for her cousins' intervention, Judith hid a smile at the pout she could hear in the child's voice. Thankfully, the rest of the meal passed without any further references to Mark. Judith was ashamed of the relief she felt when Robbie left the table after dessert to play with a computer game. "I don't suppose Leo would like to give us another little lecture on Jaguars, huh?" Judith foresaw questions coming up.

"I'm all lectured out, cuz."

"Right," she said, sighing. "I don't mind. I guess—oh, ask whatever you want. It won't make any difference, anyway."

Leo asked where Mark was. "I haven't seen... he hasn't—"

"Well, I guess I don't need a Ph.D. to know that something's wrong," Leo said. "You haven't come by cab ever since you and Mark have been an item."

"Don't push, Leo," Maggie chided.

"Like I said to Robbie, Mark's out of town. But even if he'd been back in Baltimore, I'm pretty sure I would have come alone tonight. I... it hasn't worked out," Judith admitted, her words getting lost in a cavernous silence. "You're not saying anything."

"It's your life, Judith," Leo said.

"And you're my family," Judith retorted.

"What happened?" Maggie asked. "You don't have to tell us anything if you don't want to. But Leo and I want to help you, if we can."

Judith took a deep breath, releasing it in a shaky sigh. And then she told them about the aborted trip to New York. "I just couldn't seem to make him understand how important my work was."

Leo and Maggie exchanged puzzled glances. Then Leo gestured for Maggie to speak.

"I would have thought that of all people, Mark would understand how important your painting—your art—is to you. It's the most important thing in your life, isn't it, Judith?"

"Of course not!" she replied without hesitation. "The most important thing—I mean, that is, I've been without it so long."

"What was it you started to say?" Maggie asked softly. "Truth, Jude, like we used to say when we were roommates."

She took a deep, shuddering breath. "Truth, Maggs. Mark's the most important thing in my life," Judith answered, the words spoken more to herself than to her listeners. "I love him. So much."

"Like you say, we're your family. We love you. But you do get kind of focused in on things, single-minded, to the exclusion of everything—everyone else. When's the last time you've been here, or we've been to your place, unless it had to do with the show?"

"I was working, Maggie—harder than I've ever worked in my life."

"That's no secret! We've asked you over three or four times, but you've spent all your time cloistered in your studio," Leo cut in sharply. "You're isolated from the world, Jude. Now, *we* can handle that. We're used to it. Hell, Maggie and I have each other, and Robbie. Did you ever think that maybe Mark couldn't handle being isolated from you when you're caught up in the throes of artistic genius?"

"Leo!" Maggie exclaimed.

"I'm sorry, Maggie. It's true."

"You think I'm a selfish, disgusting bitch." Judith's words were a statement, not a question. "A taker."

"You decide," her cousin replied.

"If the shoe fits…" What had she really done for Mark, Judith asked herself morosely. Forgiven him when there was actually nothing to forgive? Let him into her life? What had she given him other than her body? Was that enough? And not even that in recent weeks. She *had* cloistered herself, to use Leo's words, focusing on art to the exclusion of everything else. "I've never even told him I love him. I don't even know if he loves me." She felt Maggie's arms come around her.

"Judith, if you don't know by now that Mark loves you, then you really *are* blind! You're more than blind. You're— you're living under a rock!"

"Well put, my love, if I do say so myself," Leo said dryly.

"I guess I'm pretty hopeless, huh?" Judith muttered.

"No, you're not hopeless, or beyond redemption," Maggie said. "But I think if you want Mark, you're going to have to do something about it, like maybe learning how to compromise. It seems to me that he's already put in a king-size effort. And I have a gut feeling that if there's going to be a closer relationship, the move will have to come from you. And part of that had better be telling him what you really feel for him."

"Very subtle, Maggie."

"You may not have noticed, Leo, but subtle doesn't usually work with Judith."

"Maggie's right, Leo. I guess I was subconsciously holding back. I didn't want him to feel obligated."

"Dunce," Maggie hissed.

"Just your average coward, Maggs, scared of what'll happen once the words are said and can't be recalled."

"After this opening is over, we are going to work on getting you a transfusion. Of courage. And now, I think that your next move had better be a ride home. You have a big day tomorrow. Enough lecturing for the night," Maggie concluded.

"I guess we were pretty rough on you, huh?" Leo said as he walked her out to the car.

Judith shrugged. "Like you said, you're family." She heaved a sigh. "And much as I hated to hear them, I know the words had to be said. I just don't know what happens now."

"What do you want to happen?" Leo asked softly.

"Whatever I want, Leo, even if I *had* a courage transfusion, I couldn't tell Mark what I feel when he's three thousand miles away."

After Leo had dropped her off at home, Judith drifted aimlessly through the house, too restless to sleep, aching for one of the massages that Mark had always seemed to administer so well.

What had been driving her, she asked herself as she lay down in the cavernously empty bed. What had been keeping her at her worktable all of her days and most of her nights until she was ready to drop—to the exclusion of everything else? Was she really selfish? The words replayed themselves in her mind until sleep claimed her.

But even though she was tired to the point of exhaustion, she woke up more than once in the middle of the night, her arms around the pillow that still held Mark's scent. She hadn't been able to bring herself to change the pillowcase. Not yet.

A yawning emptiness now existed where once she had been filled with love for him. The pain was like a cold flame burning her from the inside out.

THE CRITICS' ARTICLES appeared in the papers on Saturday morning.

"Shall I read them to you?" Maggie asked as Judith was getting dressed.

"If they're bad, I may be too depressed to go to the opening." She couldn't tell Maggie that she was already too depressed to care what the reviews said one way or the other.

"They're not bad. And try to perk up, for Pete's sake. You look like you're going to a memorial service, not a gallery opening."

"Yes, Mother," Judith replied tartly.

Some articles were flattering, some not. One critic didn't like the fact that Judith's new works were nontraditional and gimmicky, too contrived and derivative, not original enough, more suitable for a hobbyist than a true artist.

"What does that turnip-brain know?" Maggie growled. "Let's see him make something out of his life as an art critic without being able to see what he's doing!"

Anger coursing through her at the critic's harsh words, Judith heard the scrunching of paper, and strongly suspected that Maggie was trashing the article. "Maybe he *can't* see what he's doing," Judith suggested. "Keep reading, Maggs. I'm all ears."

Another critic said that her work was better now than before, reflecting a greater depth of emotion, as well as an interesting use of color. Briefly, that excited her. But she couldn't help thinking how much more the articles would have meant if Mark had been there to read them to her instead of Maggie. Aside from his support, she wanted to share her triumph with him, if that's what it was to be, and not just because part of that triumph was due to him.

By the evening of the opening, Judith was numb on the outside, shaking on the inside. An army of butterflies was performing maneuvers in her stomach. "Oh, God. I'm put together with paper clips," she muttered as she entered the opening reception with Leo and Maggie.

Over the course of the evening, she drifted throughout the gallery, listening to people comment on her works. More than one person wondered aloud how the artist had managed to paint without seeing what she was doing. If it hadn't been impolite to eavesdrop, she would have told them. It had all got started with a little jar of tempera paint and a jury-rigged canvas she had never thrown away.

But by ten-thirty in the evening, her endurance and her spirits were flagging. Judith felt alone in spite of well-wishers' kind remarks and her two friends' constant presence at her side. She did her best to enjoy the opening, but the champagne seemed flat, and the crowd was making her feel claustrophobic. And in counterpoint to what should have been an evening of triumph was her crushing disappointment that Mark wasn't there to share the evening with her.

Eventually she told Maggie that she was going outside into the sculpture garden for some air, turning down Maggie's offer to accompany her. "I know my way around the gallery blindfolded, thanks to you," she quipped to the other woman.

Using her cane, Judith threaded her way through people and displays, breathing a sigh of relief when she reached the cold night air. And then she froze. She heard no sound, but her sharpened senses alerted her to a very familiar scent. She would know it anywhere—Mark's cologne. Of course, some other man might be wearing it, she told herself, bracing herself as she called Mark's name.

A beat of silence, then another—and her question was answered.

"Hello, Judith."

Her heartbeat was suffocating her. "Hello, Mark." Her words were a breathless union of hope and anxiety. A wave threatened to engulf her; she fought to maintain a cool facade as she returned his greeting. "I didn't think you were coming."

Mark couldn't be any less than honest. "You know I wouldn't have missed it for the world," he told her.

They were both wary, and tense, Judith realized—unsure of what to say or how to react. She was reminded of that time in his office, when she'd had to make the first move. She wished, oh, how she wished, that just for a brief moment, she could see his face. "I missed you."

"I . . . missed you, too."

"Are we alone, Mark?"

He glanced around at the giant shadows cast by larger-than-life works of metal and stone. "Except for the inanimate objects. Would you like to sit down?"

"Yes, please."

He led her to a stone bench, seating her first, then sitting down next to her.

The pallor of her face contrasted sharply with her long gown of black velvet. He saw her tremble. Sensing that she was cold, he slipped off his jacket and draped it around her shoulders.

She cherished the feel of it, still warm from his body. But in spite of the chill night air, she would much rather have been wrapped in his arms than in his jacket. "Thank you."

They were like strangers, he realized. It was almost as if they had never met before, had never enjoyed the greatest intimacy possible between a man and a woman. He didn't know what to do about it. He only knew that he didn't want to prolong the proximity to her that was causing him so much anguish. "Well, I don't want to keep you from the festivities," he said, getting stiffly to his feet.

She heard him shift position and without thinking grasped his arm. "Don't go. Please." Smothering a sigh, she removed her fingers as she heard him settle back onto the bench.

"The show's a success. I saw a lot of 'sold' stickers. I've been hearing good things."

"My success is yours. It was your method, after all. I should pay you for it," she said unthinkingly.

It was only with great effort that Mark managed to douse the fire of his temper. "Don't you ever dare *think* of offering me money. The method—technique—whatever you want to call it, the profits from the sale of the paintings, they're all yours, to do with as you please."

"But I owe you so much," she protested.

"You don't owe me a thing, Judith."

No, of course not, she told herself. Just the restoration of her career through his inventiveness, and her self-worth through his love. No, it wasn't love, she chided. It couldn't be. Otherwise, why was he clearly bent on ending their relationship? Finally she couldn't stand it anymore. "Why did you go away? What's wrong, Mark?" she asked softly.

Did you even know that I was gone, he asked silently. "Nothing's wrong. You're doing what you want to do. Thank God. And I guess I've done all I can do. So I decided that maybe it was better for me to leave, so that you can get on with your life."

"No," she breathed. Although she had suspected that his feelings for her had changed, it hurt to hear him put it into words. Somehow Mark had managed to weave himself into the very fabric of her existence. And his departure would leave a rent that she would never be able to fill. Greg's defection paled in comparison.

"If you want to leave, I can't stop you," she told him, forcing the words past the lump of painful tightness that had suddenly formed in her throat. "But can I at least know why?"

"It's not that I want to leave." He took a deep breath. "How do I say this without sounding like a maudlin whiner? You don't need me, Judith. There's no room in your life for me."

"How can you say that? You're the reason I started painting again. You're the foundation of my creativity."

"Words, Judith."

"No! Not just words. Before I met you, my life was...unbalanced."

"Right," he said bitterly. "There was no art in your life. You couldn't see."

"No, Mark. I mean, before the accident. There was *only* art in my life. It took precedence, center stage, over everything else."

"How did your ex react to that?"

"He didn't think I was a very passionate woman. He wasn't very demanding."

"Or very bright," Mark muttered under his breath.

"You say the nicest things sometimes. Anyway, before the accident, I was living in a kind of artistic vacuum. And then, when you gave me the opportunity to paint again, I tried to go back to my life the way it was, making everything just as unbalanced as it used to be. If there was a median, a neutral ground, I didn't know how to find it. I didn't realize until you were gone that *you* were the counterweight, the balance in my life."

"Balance?" When he'd racked his brains for a way to give Judith back her art, Mark had never known what price he would pay for his success. Now, he knew. He'd prayed that she would be able to paint. She could. "Honey, you homed in on painting like a homing pigeon. At first I thought it was just the way any creative person works.

Then I thought it was obsession. But at the end, I put it all together."

"Put *what* all together?"

"I realized that in focusing on art, you could also wipe out the past year, the time of your blindness, and everything that went with it."

"Everything? What does that mean?"

"I'm a reminder of a bad time in your life."

"Mark—"

"Yes, Judith. It's true, and you know it. I think maybe deep down, you buried yourself in your painting in order to forget what caused you to lose all that time."

"No!"

"Yes," he insisted quietly. "I gave you a ticket back to your world, but there's no place in it for me. Maybe I never belonged there at all."

"Yes, you did," she argued hoarsely. "You *do*."

"Ah, Judith," he said, sighing. "You once told me that you'd been obsessed with me, that I'd been the focus of your existence. Well, for me, it's been the same. I've been obsessed with *you*. You've been *my* focus. It will have to change now. We don't belong together, don't need each other."

"Speak for yourself. You gave me a way to paint, but that doesn't mean that the brush should exclude everything or everyone else from my life. I know that now."

"How did you find out?"

"By digging deeper into my feelings than I'd ever gone before. Deep enough to bleed."

"What did you find?"

"The first thing I found out was that my happiness didn't depend only on myself, but on another person, and that scared me. And then I dug even deeper, trying to figure out what was driving me so hard, making me work until I was ready to drop."

"I didn't think you'd noticed."

"Oh, I noticed. It was pretty hard to miss, even for me. I'd always been absorbed, but not so completely obsessed. And then you left. I took a good look at myself, and I didn't like what I'd become. I found that painting wasn't enough now, maybe it had never been enough, but I'd been too blind to know that."

"You can't change the way you do your art."

"Hey, I may not be able to see, but I'm damned tired of being blind emotionally. I didn't want to lose myself that way, but I couldn't seem to help myself. And I kept delving until I found out why."

"It's obvious. You wanted to recapture your former success."

"No."

That one word stopped him, gave him pause. He saw the way her hands twisted together. As if in a dream, he saw his hands reach out to cover hers. "What then, Judith?"

"The drive, part of it, was because I was afraid if I didn't keep painting, I would forget how. And then—"

"Go on, Judith," he urged softly.

"It—it wasn't just for me. It was for you. I was afraid that if I didn't make it as a painter—"

"Oh, honey, it doesn't matter if you paint or not."

"Mark, I was doing it for *you*. I thought if I were painting—if I were an artist again—I thought you would be able to forget the accident."

"Judith!"

"And then I hurt you, screened you out, because I got so carried away with it all, it was as if the brush were controlling me, instead of the other way around."

The next thing she knew, she was in his arms, her head against his chest.

His hand edged under the draped jacket, gently stroking her velvet-clad back. "Oh, lady, you are so special," he murmured huskily.

"I love you, Mark." Pain lacerated her as she felt him stiffen in her arms. Immediately she began to back away. "I guess you didn't want to hear that, but I'm not sorry I said the words. I love—"

He stopped her words by bringing his mouth down on hers.

The heat of his kiss turned the cold night into an inferno. When it finally ended, when breathing became a necessity of life, she was trembling in his arms, aching for him. And his body was taut as a bowstring. She could feel the heat of his rigid masculinity against the heavy folds of her gown.

But still, he had said nothing to respond to her declaration. Suddenly she could stand it no longer. "Do you . . . love me, Mark?" She was terrified of his answer.

"Of course I love you!" he panted, his eyes irresistibly drawn to her mouth, which was still wet from his kiss. "I think I've been in love with you since we shared that icy hell. It's just . . . oh, Judith, I hurt so damned much," he ground out.

"Hurt?" Anxious, she ran her hands over him, brailling his body, reading the tension she found in muscles that were steel hard. "Where are you hurt, love?"

"It's not physical. It's a combination of frustration, and pain, knowing that whatever I did—what I would ever do could never be enough."

Her fingers were at the back of his neck, gently working at the tautness she found there. "Make me understand what you mean, Mark." To her amazement, she could feel him trembling beneath her touch.

"Listen, just listen, Judith. At first, all I wanted to do was make sure that you were all right. And then I wanted you to be able to paint again. And somewhere along the way, I fell in love with you. I wanted to tell you long before tonight."

Then why was he shaking, she wondered as she put her arms gently around him. She knew his body; it was leaner than it had been. That told her what he wasn't saying—how much he had suffered. "Why didn't you ever tell me you loved me, Mark?" she asked softly. "Aside from the fact that I was too cowardly to tell you the same thing."

"Because I thought if you could paint again, everything would be—all right."

"It is. It's better than all right," she assured him.

"No, it's not. It isn't enough, any more than my devising the painting method was enough."

"Mark, that's just not true. You've given me back my painting, my career, maybe even my sanity. And so much of yourself," she added softly.

"But there's one thing I couldn't give you," he persisted doggedly.

She could hear him swallow convulsively, and longed to be able to comfort him. She didn't know how. "What was it that you weren't able to give me?" she asked gently.

"Colors. I couldn't give you colors."

Judith groaned inwardly at the despair in his stark words, and at the tension in him that she could feel being transmitted to her. Yielding to instinct, she took her free hand, and very gently let her fingers trace the sensitive area under his eyes. Where the skin was wet with tears. Then she put both arms around his neck, drawing him closer to her, pressing her slender softness into the strength of his body.

At first he was stiff, but then he sighed deeply, returning her embrace with his own, and with interest. When he kissed her, his mouth fusing with hers, her body yearned for the fulfillment to be found only when they were one. That would come later, in the privacy of her home, or his. For now, all she wanted to do was lay her head in the hollow of his shoulder, and not move for the foreseeable future. But she couldn't do that, not until she had answered his kiss—and his self-doubts—with words.

The words she chose were so clear that she could almost see them written. And they were true. She believed them with all her heart. And if she accomplished nothing else, she would make sure that the man who held her believed them, too.

"Mark, I love you more than colors."

He believed her.

They went in through the terrace door. The house was dark, most of the servants were down at the circus, and only Nelbert's hired security guards were in sight. It was child's play for Blackheart to move past them, the work of two seconds to go through the solid lock on the terrace door. And then they were creeping through the darkened house, up the long curving stairs, Ferris fully as noiseless as the more experienced Blackheart.

They stopped on the second floor landing. "What if they have guns?" Ferris mouthed silently.

Blackheart shrugged. "Then duck."

"How reassuring," she responded. Footsteps directly above them signaled that the thieves were on the move, and so should they be.

For more romance, suspense and adventure, read Harlequin Intrigue. Two exciting titles each month, available wherever Harlequin Books are sold.

INTA-1